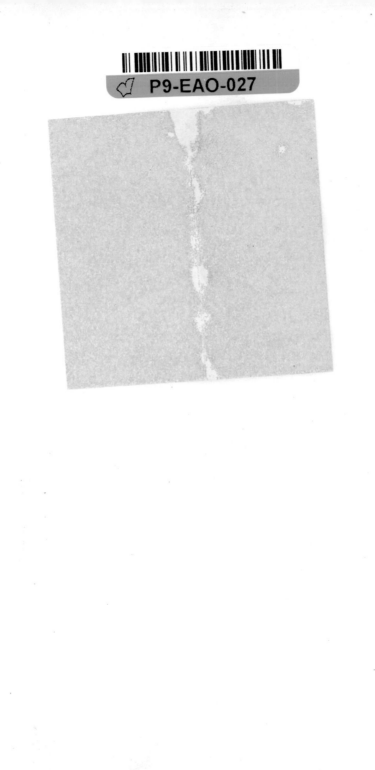

Deadly Petard

RODERIC JEFFRIES

Deadly Petard

An Inspector Alvarez novel

St. Martin's Press
New York

Library of Congress Cataloging in Publication Data

Ashford, Jeffrey, 1926-
  Deadly petard.

  I. Title.
PR6060.E43D4   1984   823'.914   83-21127
ISBN 0-312-18531-6

First published in 1983 in Great Britain by
William Collins Sons & Co. Ltd.

First U.S. Edition

10 9 8 7 6 5 4 3 2 1

CHAPTER 1

Alvarez watched the barman carefully place the small balloon glass of brandy down on the bar, next to the cup of coffee. The barman rested his elbows on the bar and his chin in the palm of his hands. 'You're not very busy at the moment?'

'Busy enough to need a break every now and then,' corrected Alvarez.

Another man entered. The barman made no move until the newcomer impatiently called for a coffee and then he reluctantly stood upright and slowly moved down the bar.

Alvarez sipped the brandy, after which he poured what remained into the coffee. He stirred in another spoonful of sugar and thought contentedly that there were now only two and a half hours to lunch and the lomo con col Dolores had said they would be eating. When his cousin cooked loin of pork wrapped up in cabbage leaves and flavoured with pine kernels, raisins, and sobrasada, it was a dish fit for a king.

The barman returned. 'How about a ticket in the lottery, Enrique?'

'Why not? I'm feeling lucky.' Then his native sense of caution returned. 'One minute—how much is it this week?'

'Five hundred for a decimo and the top prize is forty million.'

Then a winning decimo would be worth four million. Provided one kept away from the tourist areas, four million could still buy a modest finca with enough land to enable a man to earn a living. 'OK. Let's see what you've got.'

The number of one of the tickets contained three fours and four was his lucky number. It was clearly a sign from above. He paid with a five-hundred-peseta note and then carefully folded the lottery ticket in half and tucked it into the inside compartment of his wallet. He called for another brandy to celebrate his coming good fortune.

The walk back to the guardia post was a short one, but the day was sunny and the temperature was nearly twenty degrees higher than it had been recently and by the time he reached his office on the first floor he was out of breath and sweating. He hurriedly sat and as he slowly recovered he thought about the finca he would buy, with its ancient, twisted olive trees, its bountiful almond trees, rich land giving three or perhaps four crops a year when carefully irrigated . . .

The telephone on his desk rang, jerking his thoughts back to the present. 'Is that Inspector Alvarez?' asked a woman with a plum in her mouth.

'Speaking,' he answered, regretfully certain that only one woman in the world had a voice quite like that.

'Superior Chief Salas wishes to speak to you.'

Gloomily, he reflected that he could not return the compliment.

'Alvarez,' said Salas, typically not bothering with any polite social greeting, 'where the devil's your latest monthly crime report?'

Alvarez looked at the jumbled mass of papers on his desk: presumably, the form was somewhere among them. 'Señor, I have been very busy . . .'

'Does that mean you haven't yet returned it?'

'In a sense, yes. But . . .'

'Are you aware that in the past year there has not been a single month in which your report has arrived on time?'

It was not something to which he had given much thought.

'I want it in my office by tomorrow morning.'

'I will do my best, señor. But I'm very busy . . .'

'Another thing. We've received a request from England asking us to interview an Englishwoman by the name of Señorita Dean, who lives at number fifteen, Calle Padre Vives, Caraitx. You're to go and question her . . .'

'Señor.'

'What is it?'

'Caraitx is not in my department. The inspector in charge of CID there is Inspector Antignac.'

'Would it be too much to ask you to credit me with sufficient intelligence to know who is the inspector of each department under my command? The señorita is English and Inspector Antignac does not speak a word of English. Further, he already has a great deal of work in hand.'

'I, also, am a very busy man, señor.'

'You will see her and ask her if she can identify a woman by the name of Sandra who is a friend of an Englishman, Keir West. England wants to know her full name and address and any other available information concerning her.'

Alvarez wrote the name on the edge of an envelope. 'What are the circumstances of the case?'

There was a short pause. 'I am reluctant to go into much detail,' said Salas coldly, 'because experience has proved that, given the opportunity, you invariably introduce chaos into order. However, I suppose you must understand the broad outline. Señora West has died, some time ago. Her death initially appeared to be suicide, but circumstances later pointed to murder. She left a diary and while most of the entries in this were in plain language, a few of the later ones, all very short, were in a code, based on substitution. Because these entries were so short, and a different master sentence was used for each one, it has taken the experts until now to decipher them all. Every entry refers to the fact that Señora West's husband has been out with a woman called Sandra. It has

proved impossible to identify the woman and so, since
Señorita Dean has known Señor West for a long time, it is
thought she might be able to help.'

'Is she likely to prove co-operative?'

'I've no idea. But I'd remind you that one of the duties
of any competent detective is to persuade a reluctant
witness to give evidence.'

'Indeed, señor. It was just that I was wondering how
best to go about interviewing the señorita.'

'In the most efficient way,' snapped Salas, before
ringing off.

No one, thought Alvarez, as he replaced the receiver,
could ever mistake the fact that Salas came from Madrid.
He checked on the time. There were now less than two
hours to lunch so obviously there was no point in doing
anything before the afternoon. He settled back in the
chair and gradually his previous sense of contentment
returned.

During the night snow had fallen in the mountains, but
just before daybreak the wind had backed to the south to
bring clear skies and the warmth of Africa.

As he drove towards the snow-capped mountains,
starkly etched against a vivid blue sky, Alvarez thought
that, despite all the depredations of the foreigners, this
was the most beautiful island in the world. No wonder no
Mallorquin ever wanted to leave: who willingly exiled
himself from heaven? He rounded a tall earth bank to
come in sight of Caraitx. Could any other land boast
anything half so dramatically attractive as this village of
dappled brown roof tiles and honey-coloured walls,
climbing around a conical hill . . .

The roads through the village were steep and narrow
and his ancient Seat 600 creaked and groaned as it
climbed. Calle Padre Vives ran almost up to the crest of
the hill and stopped just short of the ancient, now derelict

watch-tower from which there had once flared the alarm whenever the Moors had landed and were sacking the countryside. No. 15 proved to be the last house on the right-hand side of the road. He knocked on the wooden front door. There was a longish wait before a woman opened it. He said in English: 'Señorita Dean?' And when she answered, he introduced himself.

She opened the door fully. 'Come on in.'

He entered. She was a tall woman, perhaps as much as five centimetres taller than he, and thin: but then English women were so often too thin for Mallorquin tastes. She was dressed in a check shirt and jeans and both were paint-stained: he was surprised she should dress so scruffily. She had the kind of face that Spanish cartoonists so often pictured when portraying Englishwomen — long, heavily featured, almost more masculine than feminine: horsy. She immediately struck him as an unhappy woman.

The room he'd entered was the sitting-room. Not large, it contained a few nice pieces of Spanish furniture and these, together with a couple of gaily coloured carpets, created an effect of peaceful charm. In the far corner was a semi-circular fireplace in which several logs were laid ready for firing.

'Sit down over there,' she said, pointing to the chair to the right of the fireplace. 'And would you like some coffee?'

'Thank you, señorita, but there is no need to bother.'

'It won't be any bother as I always have coffee at around this time.'

'In that case, I should very much like some.'

'Good. Excuse me, I shan't be a moment.'

She left, passing through an arched doorway across which was drawn a heavy curtain. He studied the framed painting which hung on the wall opposite where he sat. It showed sharply descending roofs, the central plain, and distant mountains and the sea, and he guessed it to be the view from the roof of this house. If she had painted it, then that would explain the condition of her clothes.

She returned, carrying a tray on which were two mugs of coffee, a sugar bowl, and a milk jug. She held the tray for him to help himself, then put it down on a glass-topped occasional table and picked up the remaining mug. She added milk to the coffee, but no sugar, sat on the armchair on the other side of the fireplace. 'Well, what brings you here?' she asked abruptly. 'Have I filled in the papers for my residencia wrongly or got the car papers in a muddle?'

'Nothing like that, señorita. I have been asked to come here and speak to you by the police in England.'

Her concern was immediate. 'What's happened?' she asked thickly. 'Has . . . ' She stopped.

He waited, but she picked up her mug and drank, making it clear that she'd overcome her first sense of shock and wasn't going to say anything more until he'd detailed the reason for the English police's request. 'I believe you knew Señor and Señora West?'

'Yes.'

'And Señora West unfortunately died?'

'She committed suicide.'

'As I understand things, the English police do not seem to be quite certain about that.'

'I don't give a damn what they're not certain about. Babs committed suicide.'

'Did you know her well?'

'No. I don't suppose I met her more than a dozen times all told.'

'You know Señor West much better?'

'Yes.'

'How long have you known him?'

'Since we were kids together. Look, what's this all

about? I've answered all these questions again and again back home.'

'I am sorry, but I have to make a full and precise report. If that is the correct thing to say?' He smiled. 'I am afraid I often mistake my words.'

'If I spoke Spanish half as well as you speak English, I'm damed if I'd ever apologize to anyone,' she said brusquely. She was not going to allow herself to be influenced by his friendly manner.

'Apparently, the señora kept a diary and in this she sometimes wrote in a code.'

'Well?'

'The English police have only just been able to decipher what was written.' He paused. 'Señorita, do you know who Sandra was?'

She stared blankly at him for a second, then started. 'No,' she said sharply. She looked away, raised the mug to her lips, found it was empty.

It seemed possible that to begin with the name had meant nothing to her, then she had remembered something. 'Señorita, can you not perhaps suggest who Sandra might be?'

'No, I can't.'

'Señora West must have either known Sandra or known of her.'

'Which doesn't mean a thing as far as I'm concerned. She'll have known dozens of people I've never even heard of.'

'Perhaps Señor West knows Sandra?'

'Perhaps.' She shrugged her shoulders.

'You cannot tell me?'

'No.'

'You have never heard him mention her name?'

'Never.'

He fingered his heavy chin. 'Are you quite certain?' he asked quietly.

She faced him and spoke defiantly. 'How definite do I have to get before you accept what I'm saying? I don't know any Sandra, I've never heard mention of Sandra, and as far as I'm concerned neither Keir nor Babs knew Sandra.'

'Then that is very clear. Thank you for your help.'

She was obviously surprised that he did not intend to pursue the matter.

CHAPTER 2

Gertrude stood in the front doorway of her house and watched the Seat 600 complete a three-point turn and carry on down the sharply sloping road towards the right-hand corner. Then she closed the door, returned to the fireplace where she put her hands on the wooden mantelpiece and leaned her brow against her hands as if trying to ease a savage headache.

Fool to believe, as she had, that her memories were buried and that her new-found happiness could last.

For she had been happy: far happier than she'd ever been before. And it had been a happiness which had been all the sweeter because when she'd first settled in the village, contrary to all her hopes the villagers had treated her with a reserve which had come close to hostility. Later she had learned that, being in the centre of the island, they met few foreigners and even a fellow Mallorquin from another village was someone to be treated with caution and doubt . . . But she'd repaid reserve with a smile, had struggled to understand and speak Mallorquin rather than Castilian, had been ever ready to laugh at herself when she made some terrible linguistic blunder . . . Few Mallorquins could resist laughter. One or two of the women had begun to talk to her when she was out shopping and others had joined in — politely, but purposefully, correcting her Mallorquin because if she was doing them the honour of trying to speak their language, they would do her the honour of teaching her to speak it reasonably correctly. And one day, as she had been walking back up towards Calle Padre Vives, a woman standing in the doorway of a house had called to her that she looked tired and she needed a cup of cocoa and an ensaimada to refresh her body and soul. For the first time, she'd entered another house in the village . . . Later, they'd learned that she painted and this gained her enormous respect: to them, there was something mystical about being able to paint . . .

And now the past had returned to haunt her.

She was upstairs in her studio when, a couple of hours later and not long after it had become dark, the front doorbell sounded. She put the stick of charcoal down, went below, switched on the outside light, and opened the front door. She gave a muffled cry when she saw Keir West, whom she'd believed to be a thousand miles away.

'That's one way of greeting an old friend!' he said with sardonic amusement.

But for the scarred area on his right cheek, he would have been too handsome: there would have been a suggestion of femininity that would have made people wonder. But the scars added a flaw which hardened his looks while at the same time they called for sympathy. So people seldom doubted him until they knew him well.

He came forward and lightly kissed her on one cheek. 'You're looking more attractive than ever Gertie.'

She remembered the first time he'd told her she was beautiful. She'd known he didn't mean it, but even so she'd experienced a sudden warmth she'd been unable to hide.

'Well, am I going to be asked in or do I spend the night

out in the cold?'

He had always been a smart dresser and he was now wearing a lightly checked suit of perfect cut and a salmon coloured shirt. His tie was green. She wondered if another man would have worn a black tie.

He stepped past her and looked around. 'I see you've gone native. Good. I knew you'd never descend to a three-piece suite and antimacassars.'

'Upstairs I've an aspidistra in a brass bowl,' she said, trying to meet mockery with mockery.

'All the rage among the smart people.'

'Why have you come here? What d'you want?'

'I'll start by accepting a strong gin and tonic. Hell, I've been travelling for days and I'm so thirsty I could drink water without being ill.'

'You've been days?'

He crossed to the fireplace and stood there with his back to it. 'You must have read about the bastards in air traffic who are going slow?'

She shook her head. 'I haven't seen a paper in days.'

'Hasn't the news been on the local goggle-box?'

'I don't have television.'

'Christ, you really have buried yourself out in the sticks!' He brought a slim gold cigarette case from his coat pocket. 'Have you taken up smoking yet?'

She shook her head.

'A pity. Indulging in at least one vice would do you the world of good.' He lit a cigarette. 'Yeah. I turned up yesterday morning at the airport only to find the flight was cancelled. No apologies, even though I was first class, just a printed notice and a girl behind the desk who couldn't have been less interested. I made 'em get me on the first available flight, though,' he said with satisfaction, remembering how rude he'd been. 'So here I am, throat like a dried-out piece of sandpaper and only kept alive by the vision of a very large, very iced gin and tonic.'

She remained where she was for several seconds, then left and went through to the small, well equipped kitchen. He'd never have come to the house unless he wanted something, she thought as she opened the cupboard in which she kept the drinks. But what could she possibly offer him now? An alibi? She'd provided that. Money? He'd inherited a fortune from Barbara. Love? What kind of a bloody fool question was that? But she knew a sudden, brief yearning.

She carried two glasses back to the sitting-room and handed him one. He raised his. 'Here's to life, Gertie: may it always deal us trumps.' He crossed to the nearest chair and sat, his legs stretched out. He had no hesitation in making himself completely at home, even to the extent of ignoring a nearby ash-tray and flicking ash into the fireplace. 'If you haven't been seeing the papers, I don't suppose you've been keeping up with the events at home?' He didn't speak quite as casually as he'd intended.

'No, I haven't.'

'You know, you surprise me, cutting yourself right off like this. But then you've made quite a habit of surprising me. Like the day you sold up at home and came out here without a word to anyone.'

'There was no one to tell.'

'There was me. I was hurt that you never said goodbye.'

'You — hurt?'

'I'm really quite sentimental at heart . . . Tell me, what made you leave so suddenly?'

'I wanted to get away.'

'Obviously. But the question is, why?'

'What's it matter now?'

He drew on the cigarette. 'You didn't begin to get doubts, did you, Gertie? That wasn't why you quit? I swear I told you the truth.'

It was strange, she reflected, how he'd always yearned

to be believed, even when it didn't matter. His one major weakness?

He threw the cigarette on to the logs and drained his glass. 'If you were to offer me a refill, I just couldn't refuse.'

She had not sat down and she now went over, collected his glass, and continued through to the kitchen.

When she returned, he reached up and gripped her right hand. 'You're quite the sweetest person I know, Gertie.'

She felt herself flushing. She tried to free her hand.

'Suppose I were to ask you to do me one last favour?' His voice was low and warm, his expression earnest. Then he cocked one eyebrow, in ironic interrogation, as Clark Gable had once done in a thousand high street cinemas when the circle seats cost two and six.

She finally managed to free her hand and she went over to a second chair and sat. 'What is it you want now?' she asked wearily.

He revolved the glass between thumb and forefinger. 'The police at home are proving to be even bigger fools than I'd imagined. D'you know, they're still convinced I murdered Babs! The bloody fools just cannot understand that I loved her and wouldn't have hurt her for anything in the world.' He was silent for a while, his eyes unfocused. Then he continued. 'I didn't see sight or sound of them for weeks and thought they'd finally come to their tiny senses. Then the other day two of 'em turned up at Middle Manor and tried to make trouble. Seems they finally managed to crack those bits in code in Babs's diary . . . Funny to think Babs could keep 'em guessing for so long when she was no master mind and they're meant to be so smart, isn't it?'

She wondered if he had the slightest inkling of how callous he sounded, talking about his dead wife in such terms?

'According to them, every single entry referred to me being out with Sandra.'

'So I heard.'

'And most of the time I was just at the club having a pint . . .' He stopped, suddenly realizing the import of what she'd just said. 'How d'you hear, when you don't get any news?' he asked roughly.

'A Spanish detective was here earlier today. He asked if I could identify Sandra or knew anything about her.'

His expression was now one of angry, panicky concern: he gripped the arms of the chair. 'Those bloody air traffic controllers: but for them, I'd have been here yesterday. What did you tell this bloke?'

'That I didn't know anyone by that name.'

He slowly relaxed: he let go of the chair. 'Did he believe you?'

'I think so. In any case, he didn't ask any more questions.'

He drank heavily.

Alvarez telephoned Palma and spoke to Superior Chief Salas. 'Regarding that request from England, señor, I have spoken to Señorita Dean.'

'Yes?'

'She says she has never known anyone by the name of Sandra and therefore cannot begin to identify her.'

'Was she telling the truth?'

'I am not certain.'

'Then she was lying?'

'I'm afraid I can't be certain of that, either, señor.'

'Typical!' snapped Salas. 'Is your report in the post?'

'I regret, not yet. After all, I have only recently returned from interviewing her . . .'

'I am referring to your latest monthly crime report.'

'Oh! . . . Señor, due to having to drive to Caraitx to question the señorita my time's been very occupied . . .'

'Are you trying to tell me you still haven't done it? Goddamn it, what do you do all day long—sleep?' Salas slammed down the receiver.

Alvarez sighed. There was no pleasing some people.

CHAPTER 3

A carriage clock struck eight. West looked at his gold Braguet wristwatch. 'I'd better be moving.' The fire had been lit and the reflected light from the flames danced across his face, occasionally highlighting the scars on his cheek. 'I don't know what time they serve dinner, but I've been told it's always late in Spain so I should still be all right by the time I get there.' He stood. 'I've booked in at the Parelona. They say it's not too bad a pub?' His voice rose, turning the last sentence into a question.

She didn't answer. He knew just as well as she that the Parelona was renowned as a hotel in the highest luxury class. He'd always had to boast.

'You'll come along one day and have lunch or dinner with me, won't you, Gertie?'

'No.'

'But it's months since I last had the fun of seeing you.'

'It's still no.'

He shrugged his broad shoulders. 'Maybe you'll change your mind later on, since I could be around for a bit. Originally I was only coming for a couple of days.' He paused, then continued. 'But when I flew out of Heathrow it was sleeting and the wind was icy enough to wreck a pawnbroker's sign. What's the point in rushing back to Siberia? Ever been in Middle Manor in winter? I'll swear it's colder inside than out. So I'm beginning to think this island might be a good place to winter on.'

'It gets cold and wet here as well,' she said hurriedly.

His right eyebrow cocked upwards. 'What's the panic? Scared I'll settle down out here for good?'

'I don't give a damn what you do.'

'I'm glad about that. Because if I did happen to see somewhere to rent that wasn't too grubby . . . I could very easily be tempted after seeing how lovely everything was this afternoon.'

Had he been captivated by the beauty of the island? Or did he want to remain close to her to make certain she did not go back on her denial that she had ever heard of Sandra?

'Well, I'll be on my way. Lovely to see you again. And you must change your mind and come and spend at least part of a day with me at the hotel. The brochure said the grub was good and the setting's supposed to be magnificent.'

He never had understood that some people simply didn't like ostentatious luxury. Even as a boy, he'd always wanted the biggest and the best so that people would see he had the biggest and the best.

When he kissed her goodbye, he made certain it was his scarred right cheek which touched her left one and he smiled when he felt her flinch. Then he said good-night and crossed the very narrow pavement to a parked green Seat 132.

She watched him start the engine, turn, and drive down the sloping road: just before he reached the corner, he put his left hand out of the window and waved.

Knowing a bitter, empty sadness, she stared out to the south, through a gap between two houses on the opposite side of the road, not really seeing the lights of villages or the distant coastline, just visible in the moonlight if one knew where to look. Did other people have to discover that happiness was always rationed and, no matter how much unhappiness one had known in the past, that ration was never sufficient?

She returned into the house, shut and locked the front door, crossed to the fireplace. The logs had almost burned away, leaving a dying, intermittent flame and glowing ashes. Soon, without more logs, there would be very little heat given off, so why not go to bed? But it was still very early. And she'd never get to sleep while her mind was such a maelstrom of memories.

She bent down and picked out a couple of logs from a cane basket and threw them on to the fire, prodded them deeper into the ashes with the toe of her shoe. She went through to the kitchen and poured herself another drink: normally abstemious, there were times when she sought, and found, a measure of comfort in alcohol.

She returned to the sitting-room and sat. She watched small, dancing flames spread along the sides of the two logs. If only the past could be burned into ashes . . .

Memory was a strange, elusive thing, sometimes strong, sometimes weak.

With only a little more talent and strength of character, her father might well have been a success in life: as it was, he had been a failure. While his wife had been alive, he had listened to her advice and had been guided by it, but after her death he had seemed to lose all sense of proportion and self-judgement.

Life had become movement. No sooner settled in one school then moved to another where she was a stranger and therefore an object of scornful interest: no sooner a friendship formed than it was forcibly sundered. They had lived in so many houses and moved so often that none of them had ever become home. They'd had few possessions and the more valuable of these — valuable? — had had to be sold from time to time to try and raise a little capital to finance more movement: the eternal quest to reach the foot of the rainbow.

And then something had happened, and she had never

learned what, which had provided them with some capital and brought an end to her father's restless wanderings. They'd rented a back-to-back in Wealdsham and lived there, month after month. No. 10, Brick Lane. A mean, ugly house in a poor street, as far as most people were concerned: a wonderful home to her.

Keir West had spoken to her only days after they'd moved in. She'd been slowly eating a Mars Bar, slowly because it was a rare treat and the pleasure had to be drawn out. He'd been so friendly that in a gesture which came straight from the heart, she'd offered him some of what remained of the Mars Bar. He'd broken off about two-thirds for himself.

His motto in life had always been a simple one: what's yours, we share; what's mine, stays mine. Once, she'd complained about his selfishness. He'd jeered at her and then she hadn't seen him for days and the loneliness taught her not to complain again.

He'd always had a precocious curiosity: a desire which was almost a need to poke his nose into everything in case he might find something of advantage to himself. So when she'd told him that her father was carrying out experiments in a room always kept locked, and that if these experiments were successful he'd make a fortune, Keir had demanded to see the room . . .

Her father had been out. She could remember getting the key from the kitchen drawer: leading the way along the dark, narrow corridor which smelled of mildew: putting the key in the lock, turning it, and opening the door: Keir pushing past her . . . But then there was a blank and no matter how much she tried to break through the mental fog she could remember nothing more until he was screaming and shrieking that she'd killed him by spilling the acid over him.

Her father, shocked that by disobeying him she'd been responsible for causing such injuries, had forced her to go to the hospital. Keir, lying in the end bed in the children's ward, had told her that the pain was so terrible he kept fainting. He didn't faint while she was there. That night she had lain in bed and prayed that she could be hurt as terribly as he'd been hurt by her, so that by her suffering his could be relieved. She had failed to experience any blinding outburst of pain.

Time had blunted her sense of guilt and increasing age had enabled her to realize that logically one could not realistically be held responsible for an accident which had happened when one was young: but her need to make amends, in so far as this was possible, had grown no less. When he wanted her to do something, she did it. Her father, casual enough over most things, had taught her a set of old-fashioned values: to steal was totally wrong. Yet when Keir had needed her as an accomplice, she had helped him steal . . . And, seemingly perversely, she had refused to make friends with others of her own age. Perhaps, subconsciously, she'd realized that had she done so, she'd have gained a far more balanced outlook and then wouldn't have been nearly so ready to follow him . . .

Her first job had been as a trainee shop assistant. Her first wage packet had been shared with him. (One could hardly have expected him not to take advantage of the circumstances.)

Her father had died suddenly and very soon afterwards Keir had left the neighbourhood, with no one knowing or caring where he'd gone. She'd experienced a crushing loneliness, but by now she found it almost impossible to make friends. Personal relationships of any depth seemed to be beyond her.

Not quite by accident, yet neither by design, she'd discovered that she had a considerable talent for painting. Her father had often told her that his grandfather had been a famous painter and she'd discounted such a story because he was a great

romanticist, but she'd suddenly begun to wonder whether
he had, after all, been telling the truth. She'd had a few
lessons from a man in Wealdsham who'd possessed some
technique but little talent, but who had possessed the
ability, and generosity of artistic spirit, to recognize talent
in others. He'd encouraged her when her self-doubts had
threatened to prevent her fulfilling her early promise and
it was he who'd persuaded her to apply for a grant to go to
an art school—something she would never have done if
left to herself.

Three months after leaving art school, she'd sold her
first painting: four years after that she'd been making a
reasonable living: and one year later Keir had re-entered
her life.

He'd developed a slick assurance: a barrow-boy made
good. He'd learned to flatter, yet sound sincere, to make
a solitary, nervous, unapproachable spinster feel like a
princess.

She'd known him as an inveterate liar, yet she'd
listened when he had told her she'd become beautiful.
(After all, wasn't beauty in the eye of the beholder, not
the mirror?) She could judge he was broke, yet did not
draw the obvious conclusion that that was why he had
reappeared. He'd moved into her flat and immediately
made himself completely at home, listing all his likes and
dislikes.

She hadn't cared how outrageous his demands were.
Love was a word that meant different things to different
people: to her, it meant being wanted . . .

He'd disengaged skilfully, yet not quite able to hide his
apprehension that she might become hysterical and make
life difficult for him. Which only showed that he'd never
even bothered to understand what kind of a woman she
was. He'd told her he was only going away because he
couldn't bear to live off her any longer and when he'd

made his fortune he'd be back and nothing would ever again keep them apart. And she had let herself believe him.

She'd become commercially very successful. She'd sold the flat and, fulfilling an ambition, had bought a cottage in the country: Queenswood Farm, three hundred years old, with oak beams, inglenook fireplaces, and a couple of inside walls still with original plaster. Eighteen months after moving into Queenswood Farm, she'd first heard that Keir was engaged to be married. The news had shocked her even if, had she been able to admit this, it should not have surprised her. Then she'd learned that his fiancée was Barbara Hardy, a very wealthy woman, from a county family, at least ten years older than himself. Whereas others had found it degrading that he should so obviously be marrying for money, not love, she had found it comforting . . .

They'd met a few times after the marriage. To her own surprise, she'd found those meetings far less emotionally charged than she'd expected: experience had hardened and taught her. Yet even so, there were times during these meetings, when he smiled at her, when he held her hand a little longer than necessary, or when he chuckled as he told one of his risqué jokes, when she experienced a moment of bitter loss.

Then, one late October morning when some trees had begun to shed their leaves and the air was heavy with the smell of damp and decay . . .

CHAPTER 4

The three upstairs bedrooms in Queenswood Farm faced north and she had had a large skylight installed in the end one to turn it into a studio. She was painting there when she heard a car drive in. She swore, hating interruptions when working.

The front doorbell rang and she crossed to her right to put down the palette, but even as she set it on the table, the front door was opened and a man shouted: 'So how's the Last Supper coming along: have you got as far as the pud?'

She recognized Keir's voice and experienced a momentary sense of panic.

In sharp contrast to her paint-stained overalls worn over an ancient sweater and jeans, he had on under a vicuna overcoat a cashmere cardigan, a roll-neck, puce coloured shirt, perfectly creased trousers and twin-coloured brogues. Depending on one's terms of reference, he was either smartly or preciously dressed.

He kissed her. She drew back quickly.

'Gertie, I'll swear you look younger every single time I see you! What's the secret? Come on, tell me: I could do with a drop of the elixir.'

He looked tired and troubled. She wondered what was worrying him? Money had usually been his only concern, but since marrying Barbara surely he'd plenty of that?

'Don't look at me in that way.'

'In what way?' she asked.

'As if you were trying to dissect my soul.'

'Where's the knife sharp enough to do that?'

He laughed, put his arm round her waist, and squeezed. 'One of the many things I so like about you is that touch of ice.'

She moved away, forcing him to drop his arm. 'D'you want a drink?'

'Have you ever heard me say no?'

She led the way into the sitting-room, crossed to the very short, very narrow passage which ran on the north side of the huge central double chimney and joined the sitting-room to the dining-room. Since the dining-room could also be reached through the kitchen, she used this passage to house the elegant reproduction cabinet in which she kept the drinks. 'What would you like?' she called out.

'A Scotch. And don't worry about making it too strong . . . Gertie, d'you mind if I use your phone?'

'Go right ahead.'

She brought out from the cabinet and put on the top two glasses, a bottle of whisky, and a bottle of sweet white vermouth. As she finished pouring the Scotch, she heard him say: 'Would it be possible to have a word with Miss Tufton?'

She added soda. He said: 'Sandra? . . . Who else d'you think it could be? . . . I'll believe that when they abolish income tax . . . Is it OK? . . . Usual time, usual place. Lots of.'

She gave herself a vermouth and soda and added a slither of lemon peel. She put the glasses on a small plated silver salver and returned to the sitting-room. He was standing by the window, looking out. He turned. 'That's all right, then, they can do a service. It's a hell of a sweat these days, isn't it, getting a car looked after? You'd think you were doing the garage the service, instead of vice versa.' He chuckled at the slight play on words. 'Well — what's your news? How are the paintings going? By the score?'

'Why not by the yard?'

'Don't take offence, Gertie. You know me — can't tell a Rubens from a Picasso. But I do like your paintings.'

'Is that intended as a compliment or an insult?'

'Come on, darling, relax. Stop taking things so seriously. You've obviously been painting too many nymphs and shepherds and need a break from such bucolic frivolities. Tell you what, lunch tomorrow at Leon's: the only nymph you're likely to run into there is the odd nyphomaniac.'

'No.'

He shrugged his shoulders. 'Have it your way. But you know what they say? All work and no play, how the hell can you stay gay?'

He'd called again a week later, after dark, so she'd switched on the outside light and waited to identify him through the hall window before unlocking the front door. When he entered, drops of water slid off his mackintosh on to the brick floor. 'By God, it's filthy outside! Rain's positively lashing down and even the ducks must be shouting uncle.' He kissed her on the cheek. 'You're looking like a million dollars. Know that?'

She knew she was her usual plain, untidy self. There was a brittleness to his manner, she thought, as if he were under considerable tension.

'Gertie, I've a confession to make. I've come to ask a favour. You will help me, won't you?'

'To do what?'

He didn't answer, but instead took off his mackintosh. 'Can I drape this over the banisters? When the good God invented rain, He got carried away with his own enthusiasm.'

'Come into the warm,' she said abruptly.

They went into the sitting-room, where a large wood and coal fire was burning.

'What will you drink?' she asked.

'Nothing for me.'

Her astonishment was obvious.

He jammed his hands in the pockets of his trousers and stood with his back to the fire. He looked directly at her. 'You know I often have a flutter on the horses?'

'No, I didn't,' she answered, as she crossed to a chair and sat.

'Of course you do,' he snapped. 'Normally, I reckon to make a couple of fivers or if the worst comes to the worst, break even, but recently the bloody nags I've fancied have been running like hobbled donkeys . . . Cutting a long story short, I've ended up owing a bloke a packet and he's the type who gets nasty if he's not paid sharp on time. You know the score. A broken arm to jog the memory.'

She was frightened by the mental picture of his being beaten up. 'Then you need some money?'

'Nothing like that. I've enough to keep him sweet.' He tapped the breast pocket of his very sharply cut sports jacket. 'The trouble is, seeing him to pay what I've got and persuading him to agree to wait a bit for the rest. He's only available at night. But Babs doesn't like being left on her own after dark and she's always wanting to know where I'm going . . .'

Perhaps Babs wasn't such a blind fool after all, she thought.

'I told her this evening I was coming to see you because I've heard you've had the 'flu and were feeling all depressed and I reckoned to cheer you up a little. She agreed that was a good idea, provided all the doors of Middle Manor were double locked. But Babs can be . . . I don't want to sound disloyal, but she can be unnecessarily suspicious and she might just take it into her head to ring and check I'm here. If she does that, will you tell her I've been with you right up until five minutes before, when I took off for Petercross to try and buy you some aspirins, you having run out of 'em? Will you do that for me?'

'Frankly, I don't like it.'

'Knowing the kind of person you are, Gertie, I'm sure you don't. But please, to help me, just this once . . . I'd hate like hell to end up in hospital.'

'All right.'

'You're wonderful, plain bloody wonderful . . . Tell you what. Just to prove I'm human, I'm going to change my mind. Can I have that drink after all?'

As she stood, she thought that he must be under an

even greater strain than she had first judged. But then he'd always been terrified by the prospect of physical pain.

CHAPTER 5

After she'd finished a painting, she always knew a period when she was so dissatisfied with the work that she considered destroying it. 'That damnable gap between intellectual intention and artistic execution.' Self-honest to a degree — except where her emotions were involved — she could always see how far short of her aims she had fallen because, however successful in a commercial sense, she was not brushed with genius.

She was mooning around the house, trying not to think of the painting on the easel upstairs, unable to concentrate on anything for long, when West drove into the yard. He parked by the wooden shed that was the garage, walked down to the garden gate, and continued on round the brick path to the front door.

When she saw the expression on his face, she drew in her breath sharply because it was obvious that something had severely shocked him. What in God's name had happened the previous night when he'd met the man to whom he owed all that money . . . ?

'Gertie . . . Oh, Christ!' he said hoarsely.

'How much does he want? I can help. I can draw it first thing tomorrow morning.' She gripped his right arm, almost pulling him into the house.

He was bewildered. 'What the hell are you talking about? It's Barbara. She's dead.'

'Dead?' she whispered.

'When I got back home last night . . .' He gulped.

She cradled him against herself and murmured words

which barely made sense, but were merely intended to soothe. 'How ghastly! How terrible! Poor Keir! Why didn't you tell me sooner? Come and sit down.'

They went into the sitting-room and she poured him out a brandy which he drank quickly and without pleasure. He wiped his lips with the back of his hand. 'At first, I thought she was just asleep . . .'

'Don't talk about it unless you want to.'

'I've got to tell someone or I'll go mad.' He turned away so that she should not see his face. He spoke in a low voice. 'I didn't get back home until just before midnight. I locked up, set the alarms, had a bit of a nightcap, and then went upstairs. I thought she might still be awake, so I looked into her bedroom . . . We've been using different bedrooms for a while now. She's not a good sleeper.'

She hated herself for knowing a moment's pleasure at the knowledge that they had slept in different bedrooms.

'The bed's not far from the door and so although there wasn't a light on in the room, the light from the passage reached the bed. She was lying on her back, facing the ceiling and I decided she was fast asleep. I was just about to close the door again when I realized her face was shiny in a way I'd never seen before. So I went right in and when I got close I saw . . . I saw that there was a plastic bag right over her head.'

'Oh my God!'

'I tore it off and tried to hear her heart. I thought I could. I started mouth-to-mouth resuscitation. When that didn't do any good, I phoned the doctor. When he came, he said she was dead.'

'Oh, Keir,' she whispered, wishing there were some sacrifice she could make that would ease his sorrow.

He suddenly stood, crossed to the window, and stared out at the winter-sodden garden. 'The doctor told me she'd been dead some time before I got back. We found a note. She said she knew she was dying from cancer of the womb and couldn't bear to face the agony, so she was taking some of her sleeping pills and then killing herself with a plastic bag . . . But she didn't have cancer of the womb: the doctor tried to assure her of that a couple of weeks ago. But she wouldn't believe him or the gynæ specialist. If only I'd realized just how terrified she'd become. But she'd so often believed she was suffering from something that I'd reached the point where I didn't take nearly as much notice as I should . . . She was always seeing the doctor with new pains. One day he asked her if her marriage was unhappy. The bastard!' He swung round. 'Of course, she told him it was perfectly happy. No one could have been happier than we were.'

He walked back to the nearest chair and slumped down on it. I thought it was the end of the world. Nothing could be more terrible. And yet . . .'

'What, Keir?'

His voice became harsh. 'You know Mavis?'

Just for a moment she couldn't think who Mavis was. Then she remembered the 63-year-old battle-axe of a woman who'd first worked at Middle Manor as a scullery maid between the wars, immediately after leaving an orphanage. 'What about her?'

'She accused me of murdering Babs.'

'That's impossible!'

'When she turned up at half past eight I told her what had happened and she almost fainted. So I helped her into the kitchen. The next thing was, she was shouting that I'd murdered Babs.'

'She was hysterical.'

'She meant it. She really believed I'd murdered Babs. She told the police that.'

'Oh my God!' She tried to find the words which would enable him to understand how this had probably happened. 'Keir, you've got to remember that she went straight from the orphanage to Middle Manor so the

place became a kind of home to her: and Barbara's
mother, so someone told me, was wonderfully kind to her.
In a way, she must have felt herself part of the
family—it's the kind of relationship which just can't
happen these days. Barbara was the last member of that
family, so when Mavis heard she'd just died it must have
felt almost like having a daughter die.'

'All right, so she had a shock. But why start shouting to
the police that I murdered her when she must have known
that I wouldn't touch a hair of Babs's head?'

Obviously, he hadn't begun to understand what she'd
been trying to tell him, but perhaps in the circumstances
it was ridiculous to have expected him to do so. 'When she
gets over the shock, she'll realize she's been stupid.'

'That's all very fine, but in the meantime I've got the
police asking questions.'

'How d'you mean?'

'They're trying to discover if maybe I did murder
Babs.'

'But you can't have done. You said she left a note
saying she was killing herself.'

'I know. It's vicious. As if I hadn't suffered enough. But
I've had a detective in the house for over two hours,
asking questions, taking away things he says will have to
be examined by experts. I've had a pathologist examining . . . examining Babs. And there was another
policeman taking photos. All this because of that stupid
bitch, Mavis.'

'Oh, Keir,' was all she could find to say.

He looked across at her, his expression haggard. 'The
detective wanted to know where I was last night at ten.
That's when they think she . . . died. He was trying to
check up on me.'

'Then all you had to do was tell him about seeing that
man and he'll know Mavis's accusation is ridiculous.'

He shook his head. 'I couldn't find the bloke. He wasn't

in any of his usual places.'

'But lots of other people must have seen you?'

'No one I knew, so I can't name anyone.'

For the moment, she was nonplussed.

'Gertie, I told the detective that I was with you all evening.' His voice sharpened. 'You've got to back me up. You know it's crazy to think I could have begun to hurt Babs. If you tell the police I was here until just before midnight, they'll realize Mavis has to be out of her mind and Babs really did kill herself. Please, please, you've got to do that for me. I just can't stand any more of their filthy questions . . .'

'Yes, of course.' she said immediately.

'God, if only you could know how much that means to me!'

Detective-Constable Cullon was a few years younger than she and three inches taller: he had a rugger player's shoulders: his hair was light brown and sufficiently curly to prevent any brush or comb bringing much order to it: he had deep blue eyes set above a hawkish nose: his mouth was firm and tilted towards laughter: he looked a man who was conscientious and determined, but who knew how to enjoy life when given the chance: he also looked tired.

'Sorry to bother you, Miss Dean,' he said as he stepped into the hall of Queenswood Farm. 'I hope I'm not disturbing anything?'

'No, not really.'

'Good.' His tone altered. 'Have you heard the very sad news about Mrs West?'

'Yes, I have.'

'I understand you're a friend of the family?'

'I am, but I know Keir very much better than I ever knew Barbara.' He could make what he liked of that, she thought: in any case, having met her, he was not very likely to imagine there had been a passionate liaison between Keir and herself. He wasn't to know how things had been years ago . . .

'Mr West said you'd known each other since you were children?'

She suddenly realized they were standing about in the hall and she suggested they went into the sitting-room.

He stared appreciatively at the inglenook fireplace, then up at the beamed ceiling. 'You've a lovely old house here, Miss Dean.'

'But hardly to be compared to Middle Manor,' she retorted.

'Middle Manor is like something out of a film set. But this house is . . . Hope you don't mind me saying this, but it's much more down to earth. I can imagine myself one day owning a place like this, given a bit of luck. That makes it more attractive to me . . . Now, you won't want to be bothered with me any longer than's absolutely necessary.' He brought a notebook out of the right-hand pocket of his sports jacket, flipped it open, and looked down at it. 'I know it'll be distressing to discuss Mrs West's death, but I can assure you that it's necessary. There are just one or two points which have to be made clear.'

'Because of what Mavis said?'

'Among other things.'

'She was hysterical.'

'Quite possibly. But you'll understand, Miss Dean, that whatever the mental state of the person concerned — up to a point — when an accusation like this is made we have to investigate it. Did you happen to see Mr West at any time yesterday?'

'He was here during the evening.'

'At about what time?'

'He arrived around six: either a little before or a little after.'

'And can you say when he left?'

'Roughly midnight.'

'And was he here, in this house, all the time in between?'

'Yes.'

'Was there anyone else present?'

'No.'

'So you can offer no corroboration?'

'Are you calling me a liar?'

'God forbid!' He looked up and grinned. 'Sorry if I sounded that rude. The trouble is, we have to double-check everything and sometimes forget what that sounds like to other people.' He brought a ballpoint pen out of his breast pocket and wrote briefly in the notebook. He looked up again. 'I'd be grateful for a few impressions. Would you say Mr and Mrs West had a happy marriage?'

'As far as I know, it was perfectly happy.'

'Mrs West came from a very old family, didn't she?'

'Yes.'

'I don't suppose Mr West is from quite the same background?'

She was silent.

'Where did he live when you first knew him?'

'In Wealdsham.'

'Which part exactly?'

'A road near Brick Lane: I don't remember the name.'

'That would be east Wealdsham, wouldn't it: beyond the river?'

He obviously knew that Brick Lane had been then, as it was now, on the edge of the slums.

'You've kept in touch from time to time?'

'Yes.'

He studied what he'd written, then snapped the notebook shut. 'Thanks a lot for all your help, Miss Dean.'

She went with him to the front door and watched him walk along the brick path and out of sight around the corner of the house. He must be a fool, she thought, to place the slightest credence in Mavis's ridiculous accusation.

CHAPTER 6

Two weeks passed before she saw West again and during that time various rumours reached her, largely through Mrs Randall who came three times a week to do the housework. According to these rumours, Barbara had been murdered by gypsies, had not died but had been revived in hospital, had been murdered by West who had been arrested and confessed, had committed suicide, and Mavis had been arrested for making wild accusations . . .

West opened the front door of Queenswood Farm and stepped inside. 'Hullo, Gertie.'

She was shocked by the change in his appearance. Gone was the arrogant, smooth, slick self-satisfaction: now, he looked nervous and uncertain.

She offered him coffee and they drank it in the dining-room, sitting at the small reproduction refectory table. Outside one of the windows a length of creeper, disturbed by the wind, kept tapping on the glass.

'The police . . .' He stopped.

'What are the police doing?'

'They're convinced Babs didn't commit suicide.'

'How can they be when she left that note?'

'They say it was forged.'

'My God! . . . But why do they think that?'

He shrugged his shoulders. 'The experts say they're pretty certain the letters were individually traced out of her diary and then put together to make up the message. They're accusing me of having forged it.'

'But why you?'

'Because if it was forged, the forger either lived in the house or else knew a hell of a lot about it.'

'It's ridiculous to think you could have done such a thing.'

'They don't understand. They won't understand. I loved her. When I realized that it was a plastic bag over her head . . . It was as if someone had stabbed me. When the doctor told me she was dead, part of me died.'

'Oh, Keir!'

His voice rose. 'Because I'm younger and wasn't rich they're saying I married her for her money. But I'd have married her if she hadn't had a penny and lived in a council house. And how was I supposed to know she intended changing her will, leaving the estate to that snooty cousin of hers just because he's a Hardy and the family solicitors had finally persuaded her that it ought to stay in the family. Those bloody solicitors have been against me from the day our engagement was announced. They tried to prevent her making the will in the first place . . . I didn't begin to know she'd a draft copy of the new will among her papers — never went near her personal papers. I didn't even know she'd been to see the solicitors.'

'Keir.'

'What?'

'Why did she let the solicitors persuade her to change her mind?'

'Christ, you sound like the police!'

'I'm sorry. I was just wondering.'

He said bitterly: 'It was that bitch Mavis again.'

'You surely didn't do anything to her?'

'Like belt her one? I'm not that stupid, even if I was tempted every time she was rude to me. The old fool overheard something and told Babs, who didn't understand.'

'What kind of something?'

'It's just that a man sometimes needs a change of scene.

It's the way he's made. But it doesn't mean anything really. I didn't love Babs any the less.'

'You were seeing another woman?'

'A touch of variety, that's all. Ships that pass in the night. And Babs wouldn't have known a thing if Mavis hadn't left her specs in the kitchen and come back to find 'em. That's how she heard me on the phone.'

'Then she knew who you were talking to?'

'Not by name. But it was obvious I wasn't having a chat with the vicar.'

'And the police know about this?'

'D'you imagine Mavis would keep that sort of news to herself?'

God, what a mess! she thought. 'Keir, I know I don't really understand things, but surely if you weren't in the house when Babs died you can't have had anything to do with her death?'

'Of course I bloody can't.'

'Then you must find someone who saw you that evening.'

'I've told you a dozen times, I didn't see anyone I knew. That's why I had to get you to cover for me.'

'But I don't know that I can go on doing it. Things are different now, aren't they? Before, it was just a case of helping you and making the police see that Mavis was hysterical. But if they really do believe Barbara was murdered . . . You've got to tell the truth.'

'I daren't,' he said, his voice hoarse.

She studied him. 'You were lying to me, weren't you?' she said bleakly.

He nodded.'

'Why?'

'Because . . . because I wasn't paying any gambling debts, I was seeing a woman. And I was scared that if you knew that, you wouldn't agree to help me if Babs rang to check where I was.'

'All right. Then now you've got to go and tell the police you were out with this woman. When they've checked up, they'll stop suspecting you of murder.'

'You still don't understand. They heard from Mavis about that phone call. If now they can prove I went on seeing another woman — a lot younger than Babs and showy — they'll reckon my motive for murder was even stronger.'

'But if you can prove that the two of you weren't anywhere near Middle Manor at the time of Babs's death?'

He spoke in almost a whisper. 'But we were. Sandra lives in Exhurst. We had a meal at the Horse and Crown motel and then drove back to her place: we passed within a couple of miles of Middle Manor.'

'Oh my God! . . . But if she swears you were together all the time, didn't stop, didn't go into the house . . . ?'

'And you think the police will believe her?'

'You expected them to believe me when I told them you were here.'

'There's a hell of a difference. You're obviously reliable, but Sandra . . .' He tailed off into silence.

Is young and pretty, she thought bitterly.

Detective-Inspector Rifle was a tall, thin, austere-looking man in his early forties who never asked anyone to work harder than he was prepared to do himself: which was no consolation. He had a sense of humour, but this was so dry that many people thought he was without one. 'Miss Dean, I wonder if you quite understand the seriousness of the situation?'

Gertrude looked across her sitting-room at the detective-inspector, who sat to the right of Cullon. 'I'd have to be very stupid not to.'

'Mrs West was almost certainly murdered.'

'But you can't be positive that she was?'

He considered the question. 'Perhaps I can best answer by explaining that unless a policeman can go into a court of law and prove all the facts to the satisfaction of that court, he cannot claim to be certain in the legal sense . . . I have not the slightest doubt that Mrs West did not commit suicide, but was murdered, yet at this moment I cannot legally prove that . . . This is one of those cases where motive, opportunity, and the provable facts, all point in one, and only one, direction. Motive.' He held up one finger. 'Throughout our investigations, which have been very detailed, we have only uncovered one motive for Mrs West's murder and that is money. She was a wealthy woman and her estate will be, by anyone's standards, a very large one. So we have to ask ourselves who stands to benefit from her death? And having identified that person, we have to go on to ask whether there were intended any change of circumstances likely to produce a situation where the death of the victim becomes necessary now rather than later if the suspect is to continue to benefit.

'Opportunity.' He held up a second finger. 'By far the greatest proportion of all murders are committed by persons well known to the victim—the motive more readily arises and the routine of the murdered person is known. So if in addition a careful and sophisticated attempt is made to conceal the murder, such as presenting the death as suicide, then one immediately looks at those persons who were closest to the victim.

'The facts.' He held up a third finger. 'The facts, negative just as much as positive, all point to one person, and only one person, as having been the murderer.' He paused. 'I must amend that. All but a single fact point to one person.

'Miss Dean, I am very well aware that there can be personal factors which severely strain a person's judgement. But nothing should be allowed to obscure the fact that this murder was the deliberate taking of life, in cold blood, for gain.'

There was a long silence.

Rifle looked at Cullon. Cullon said: 'Miss Dean, last time I saw you I asked you whether Mr West was with you at any time on Tuesday, the second of November. You told me that he was here from around six in the evening until roughly midnight. Remembering all that Mr Rifle has just said, would you like to alter your evidence?'

'No,' she replied, her voice harsh.

CHAPTER 7

It had been a morning of low, dirt-washed clouds, icy wind, sleet, and occasional snow flurries: a day when the world had gone into mourning for a departed sun.

West phoned at nine-thirty in the morning. 'Have they been again?'

'No,' Gertrude answered wearily.

'You're sure?'

'For God's sake, what sort of question is that? Of course I'm sure.'

'The last time — you swore I'd been with you all evening?'

Her voice rose. 'Yes. Yes. Yes.'

'Why the hell won't they realize the truth? Babs committed suicide. She left a note, didn't she, saying that's what she intended? The post mortem showed she'd had some sleeping pills. There was a whole load of plastic bags of the same size in the kitchen. If Mavis weren't so bloody vindictive . . .'

He finally brought the call to an end. She replaced the receiver and returned upstairs. The sleet, driven hard by the gusting wind, was pounding on the window of the studio, rendering much of the glass opaque and grossly distorting the images of what was visible beyond: the electric fan heater was failing to keep the room comfortably warm, largely because there were so many draughts in the roof: her latest painting, on the easel, was wrong . . .

Goddamn Keir! she thought with painful bitterness. Why couldn't he have learned from the past to understand and measure the depths of her loyalty?

Sandra? Was she very beautiful? Or just brassy? And he'd had the filthy nerve to come to Queenswood Farm and demand a false alibi because this whore wouldn't or couldn't give him one . . .

She suddenly picked up a palette knife and repeatedly slashed the painting on the easel. Then a measure of reason returned. She dropped the knife on to the floor, crossed to the sleet-covered window, and stared out at a world of suspicion, disloyalty, and bitter loneliness . . .

Into her mind there came the memory of a fortnight's holiday in sun-drenched Mallorca. Cloudless skies: people who smiled: people whose warmth of spirit could never be mistaken . . .

Why not? she suddenly wondered. Why not escape from all the bitter, painful memories and find a new life out there?

CHAPTER 8

West stood beyond the shade of the patio on Ca'n Absel and the hard sunshine enfolded him. According to the overseas programme on the radio, it was raining in most of the UK. Cause for ironic amusement to think that but for Gertie, so calvanistic in her attitudes, he'd be back there, shivering, instead of enjoying all the hedonistic pleasures of this island . . .

He lit a cigarette. A man had a right to feel good when he rented — at a rent which made people whistle — a luxuriously equipped house with a large swimming pool and mature garden, and he owned a Mercedes 280CE, a Seat 127, and a Hatteras 53-foot motor yacht: and when, held through a company set up in Jersey to escape taxes, he had over a million and a half in securities. None of the local expatriates could ever mistake him for a poor man.

He looked down at the garden. Because the mountains were only half a kilometre away, the land was terraced, with drystone walls. The first terrace was crescent-shaped and the swimming pool had been built at the part where the land was at its widest. The pool was in two halves, both circular, one shallow and one deep: by the latter was a diving board with two heights and a water chute. Beyond the pool was a lawn of gama-grass. Lawns were a complete luxury because they needed so much water. Ca'n Absel's water came from a spring up in the mountains and was brought down along stone water channels, said to have existed since Roman times, which divided and divided again to serve all the farms in the area. The agent who'd rented him the house had told him that at one time the right to water had caused violent arguments and three men had been killed in less than fifty years — now, a general agreement had been reached over how many hours' water each property was entitled to. Ca'n Absel's share was from 9.00 p.m. Sunday night to 6.00 a.m. Monday morning. If ever the estanque into which the water fed looked too empty he'd tell the part-time gardener to divert the water whatever the day or hour. To hell with the peasants. He wasn't going to suffer a brown lawn or wilting plants.

Below the first terrace was a second and much larger one and here there grew a large number of orange and lemon trees, together with fig, pomegranate, loquat,

grapefruit, tangerine, and walnut trees. He was quite the
farmer. The thought amused him.

A car turned the corner of the dirt track to come into
view and he recognized Charlotte Payne's Seat 600. Payne
by name, pain by nature. But she was the widow of a
colonial governor, which placed her among the local
society so she was a useful person to know until such time
as he could afford to ignore her.

She parked by the side of the garage and he hurried
forward to open the driving door. She was a stickler for
good manners. He was rewarded by a kiss on each cheek.
'Good morning, Keir,' she said, in her high-pitched,
heavily cultivated voice. 'I hope I'm not interrupting
anything important?'

'In fact, nothing at all. And even if you were, I'd still be
delighted to see you.'

She had reached the age where honeyed words from a
younger man were all the more precious for being rare. 'I
couldn't ring you because I'm still not on the phone. It's
simply months now since I applied to be connected and
paid thousands of pesetas. The bongoes really are
incredibly dilatory and slack.'

'You've surely heard about the Mallorquin student who
wanted to become an efficiency engineer? No one knew
what he was talking about.'

'How absolutely true! . . . Keir, I'm giving a little party
tomorrow night and wondered if you'd care to come
along?'

It would be a boring evening, with no snappy little
blondes to quicken the blood, but socially it would be an
important party. 'I'd love to — many thanks . . . And since
you're here now, let's have a drink to get us into practice?'

'Isn't it rather early?' she asked.

He ushered her to a patio chair, under the shade of
overhanging vines, and then went into the sitting-room,
cool because of air-conditioning. 'Francisca,' he shouted.

Francisca was nearing thirty. Quite tall for a Mallorquin, she had a heavily featured face, relieved by lustrous dark brown eyes. Her husband had recently been killed in a car crash, leaving her to bring up a newly born son.

'Bring out a bottle of champagne, two glasses, and some olives,' he said.

'Yes, señor.' She understood simple English, but spoke it with considerable difficulty and with an accent that often changed words almost beyond understanding.

He returned to the patio. Charlotte was staring out at the distant bay and so was in profile to him. No wonder the natives in the country of her husband's last posting had demanded independence, he thought as he sat. He asked her if she knew how a mutual acquaintance was and, as he'd expected, was immediately regailed with the latest discreditable gossip.

Francisca came out, carrying a tray on which was a bottle of champagne together with two fluted glasses and a small smoked glass bowl containing olives stuffed with anchovies. She put the tray down on the table. 'Is all, señor?' she asked.

'That's the lot.' It was one of his proud boasts that he hadn't learned a single word of Spanish.

He picked up the bottle, stripped off the gold foil, unwound the wire cap, eased out the cork, and filled the two glasses. He handed Charlotte one, raised his own. 'As they say where I come from, "To wine, women, and song. If the first is mature, not young, and the second is young, not mature, the third can be what the hell it likes." '

Privately, she was not surprised that where he came from people should say things like that. 'I hear you were at the Weightsons the other evening?'

'Rather a good party, I thought.'

With just a quick twist of the mouth, she managed to convey the fact that she knew he was merely being polite.

'Incidentally, the Talletons were talking about you: said how much they admired you.'

She was gratified. She finished her drink and approved of the speed with which he refilled her glass, without causing her embarrassment by asking if she wanted any more.

'Apparently they knew your husband when he was working.'

'In the service,' she corrected. One thing needed to be made clear. 'As a matter of fact, we didn't see very much of them because they were commercial.' She helped herself to a couple of olives. 'I do hope the women who put the anchovies into these are always made to wash their hands in antiseptic before they start work. One doesn't want to catch their horrible diseases.' She ate. 'Was Rosalie at the party?'

'She was there, yes.'

'I think she's a charming gal,' she said graciously.

He smiled, but made no comment.

She was annoyed that he had not the breeding to confide in her whether they were now engaged, as gossip claimed. Then she drank and her sense of resentment was borne away on the bubbles.

Being almost in the geographical centre of the island and therefore far from the sea, few foreigners lived near Caraitx. Which was one of the attractions for those who chose to do so. However, they weren't necessarily completely anti-social, merely choosey, and Gertrude saw quite a lot of Bruno Meade, Norah, and Liza. Their carefree, frankly amoral way of life was so different from anything she had experienced before that this in itself was an attraction — albeit, she wasn't quite certain that it should be — and in any case she liked them a lot.

She was in the kitchen of No. 15, Calle Padre Vives, preparing a salad for her lunch, when she heard the front door crash open. There was a shout: 'Where the hell are you?'

'In the kitchen.'

'There's been a bloody calamitous catastrophe.' Meade walked through the sitting-room, his flip-flops slapping noisily on the tiled floor. 'It's a fiesta and all the shops are shut and we've run out of booze. What have you got?'

'Tomato juice and some tonics.'

'That's not even funny.' He appeared in the doorway of the kitchen. Just over six foot one tall, he had a pair of shoulders so massive that at first he appeared to be of only medium height. His hair was black and tightly curly, his eyes deep blue, his nose Roman, his lips full, moist and sensuous, and his beard luxuriant. No woman ever made the mistake of trusting him.

He stepped into the kitchen, peered into the olive-wood salad bowl into which she was grating raw carrot, and helped himself to several pieces of lettuce.

'That's my lunch you're pinching.'

'Norah's cooking lechona and you're noshing with us.'

'I ought to finish my work . . .'

'Why?' He helped himself to more lettuce.

She made no answer. On the island, there was always tomorrow.

'Right,' he said, through a mouthful of lettuce, 'where's all the booze?'

She pointed to one of the small cupboards. 'What there is, is in there. But I really haven't very much.'

He opened the cupboard door. 'No brandy!' He turned and glared at her. 'What is this — a bloody teetotallers' hall of residence?' He looked back, reached in and brought out in succession two bottles of red wine, one of white, and a half-full bottle of gin. 'Sodding fiestas! How in the hell are we supposed to know the shops will be shut today because some saint managed to get himself burned to death?'

'You could always brush up your religious knowledge.'

'Booze shops ought to be made to open, fiesta or no fiesta . . . Find a box for these while I go up and see how your latest daub's coming on.' He turned and left.

She found a large cardboard box and packed the four bottles in this, then continued grating the carrot on to what lettuce was left: the salad would do for supper.

He came down the stone stairs and began shouting as he crossed the sitting-room. 'Everything's too regular. Makes it look like some stockbroker's garden in Weybridge.'

As always, initially she resented his harsh, exaggerated criticism, then was forced gradually to admit that there might be some merit in it.

He saw the cardboard box on the table and picked it up. 'Come on, then. We've not got all bloody day to waste.'

He drove as he lived. Why he had never had a serious road accident was one of the minor mysteries of life.

The house, which lacked piped water and electricity, lay up a long dirt track which ran through farmland. It was in a poor state of repair, but the stone walls were over a metre thick and so it was dry in winter and cool in summer, in direct contrast to most houses now being built.

Norah was cooking and Liza was decorating some pottery. They were both honey-blonde, blue-eyed, proudly busted, slim-waisted, long-legged, and twenty-three. In so far as anyone could judge, they normally shared Meade without the slightest discord ever creeping into their relationships. Only if Liza had to do the cooking, or Norah the washing-up, was there any sign of discontent.

'She'd no brandy,' said Meade in tragic tones. 'Only a smell of gin and some vino. Where are the glasses, then?'

'On the kitchen table,' replied Liza.

'Get four.'

She ignored him and crossed to welcome Gertrude with a kiss on each cheek.

Norah came to the doorway of the kitchen. 'Hullo, Gertie. Everything OK? . . . Grub's up in a quarter of an hour.'

'It'll wait until we're bloody well ready for it,' shouted Meade.

She shrugged her shoulders.

Meade pushed past her to go into the kitchen, returning with four tumblers. He filled them, without asking what anyone would like to drink. Norah sat cross-legged on a rush mat and lit a joint. He leaned over and took it out of her mouth and smoked it. Without any show of resentment, she fetched herself another.

They ate at half past three, by which time the sucking-pig was grossly overdone and the roast potatoes were cannon balls. They drank the bottle of white wine with some tinned peaches and Meade emptied a bottle of maraschino into their four tumblers.

He belched, patted his stomach affectionately, and spread himself out on one of the very decrepit chairs. 'Gertie, when we were talking about Keir West once, didn't you say you'd known him back home?'

The question surprised and upset her. 'Yes,' she answered.

'Is he rich?'

'He is now.'

'Thought he must be.'

'He's very good-looking, except for all those scars on his cheek,' said Norah.

'Makes him look like a pirate,' said Liza. Her voice became dreamy. 'I love pirates.'

'Watch it!' Meade threatened.

Liza smiled.

'I've been wondering.' He put his little finger in his

right ear and began to work it around. 'I've been
wondering, if he is the bloody, pompous, ingratiating,
snobbish shit he undoubtedly is . . .' He removed his
finger and examined what he'd captured.

'Well?' said Norah.

'If he is, then what the hell's Rosalie thinking about?'

'What's the matter with Rosalie?' Gertrude asked with
sharp worry.

'I mean, she may be French, but she's all right.'

'Why's Rosalie anything to do with him?'

He began to explore his left ear with his other little
finger. 'How can she begin to consider marrying a bloody
little creep like him?'

Until she had come to live on the island, it had been
virtually true to say that Gertrude knew a number of
people but had not a single friend. Those early years of
friendships laboriously made only to have them broken
almost immediately when they moved, that childish sense
of guilt which had demanded she did not betray her guilt
by becoming friendly with anyone but Keir, that adult
uneasiness, the belief that other people must find her
gauche and boring, had all inhibited her ability to give of
herself. But in Caraitx she had found a freedom of self
and had discovered how to reach across to others. And
this had been truest where Rosalie Rassaud had been
concerned. Her friendship with Rosalie was all the
stronger because of the past blank years. Typically,
Meade had once demanded to know if the relationship
were a lesbian one. Instead of being outraged and
humiliated, she'd laughed — which proved just how much
she'd changed. But on another occasion he'd accused her
of behaving like a mother towards a daughter and this
time she'd been upset and annoyed, much to his evident
satisfaction. Had he known a great deal more about her
past life, and had he stopped to think, he might then have

suggested, with some justification, that what she was really doing was behaving like a mother to the image of herself as she might have been . . .

She crossed the floor of her sitting-room and switched off the record-player. Normally, she loved Beethoven, but now the music was interrupting her thoughts. Bruno might be wrong: he so often was. But it was true that recently she had not seen as much of Rosalie as usual and when they did meet Rosalie showed a reserve which had not been there before. Until now, she'd put all this down to the fact that Rosalie was having to face up to the toughest part of her husband's death, coming to terms with it emotionally, but what if it wasn't that at all, but was because Rosalie had fallen in love with Keir . . . ?

Keir was rotten. So rotten that on the night his wife had committed suicide, driven to do so at least in part by his promiscuous behaviour, he'd been out with another woman. But however rotten—or was it in part because he was rotten?—he could make himself very attractive to women. Rosalie was not someone who would ever find wealth a good substitute for love, but being very reasonable she would probably see it as a reinforcement of love.

Gertrude began to pace the floor, her mind racing. Rosalie mustn't suffer a second tragedy and have her life ruined by marrying Keir. He must be forced to give her up.

CHAPTER 9

Gertrude parked by the garage of Ca'n Absel, climbed out of the car, and began to walk towards the front door.

'What a very welcome surprise!'

She turned and looked down to see West by the swimming pool.

'The water's eighty-four and feels like a maiden's caress. Come and have a swim.'

'No,' she answered harshly.

'Why ever not? Not brought a costume? You've surely been on the island long enough to lose all your puritanical mores? Tell you what, if you won't go in skinny, I'll lend you a pair of trunks. It's my considered opinion that you're one of the few fortunate women who can go topless with honour.'

'Is anyone here?'

His expression became perplexed. 'When you say anyone . . . For a start, I'm here.'

'I mean, anyone else?'

'Francisca's in the house, working. Rather, I'm paying her to work. The difference is usually quite obvious.'

'I've got to talk to you.'

'Talk away.'

'Not like this: not when I have to shout.'

His expression was now one of mild curiosity. He pulled a pair of sandals on to his feet, stood. He walked round the pool, across the pool patio and the grass, and climbed the steps to the house patio. 'This is not only a welcome surprise, it's also an astonishing coincidence. Only this morning I was thinking about you and how it was high time you came and had a meal. Never clap eyes on you these days. I suppose you're not on the phone yet?'

'I haven't applied to be.'

'How you can willingly bury yourself away in the middle of a village of half-witted peasants beats me. Still, as the manager of the liquorice factory said, it takes all sorts to make the world . . . Now, a glass of champagne?'

'I haven't come here to drink.'

'That alone sets you apart from most of the other expatriates. You're still very English, Gertie.'

'And you never were.'

He grinned. 'A touch of the old asperity . . . Where

shall we sit? Out here, or inside where it's so much cooler?'

'I don't care.'

'Then let's try inside. I've been sun-bathing for so long I'm beginning to feel rather like a strip of biltong.'

He led the way under the vines, then held the door open for her to enter the sitting-room. After the fierce heat outside, the air-conditioned room initially felt frosty.

'You'll change your mind now and have a glass of bubbly, won't you?'

'I don't want anything.'

'That places me in something of a quandary. As the perfect host, perhaps I ought to join you in abstinence. But I have to confess that even when the spirit's very weak, the flesh remains all too willing.' He left by the far doorway.

When he returned, a glass of champagne in one hand, she was still standing. 'There's no extra charge for sitting, you know.'

'Is it true?' she demanded fiercely.

'If anyone on this island said it, probably not.'

'Are you engaged to Rosalie?'

His expression changed and sharpened. He smiled, raised his glass in conventional greeting, drank. He crossed to one of the luxurious armchairs and sat.

'Well? Are you engaged to her?'

'Gertie, why so concerned?'

'You can't.'

'I can't what?'

'You can't marry her.'

'When you say "can't", what are you envisaging? That when the vicar asks if anyone knows of any just cause or impediment someone will pop up and shout "Yes". I've always thought it would be great fun to be present when that happened, but I must confess I'd rather the wedding in question was not my own.'

'She's much too good for you.'

'Now isn't that becoming a little unkind to me?'

'You can't marry her after all that happened in England.'

'Did something in particular happen in England?'

'You know what I mean,' she shouted. 'Barbara's suicide.'

'That was very tragic. And it's taken me a long, long time to get over it. But I've never believed one should allow any tragedy, however great, to blight the whole of the rest of one's life. After all, were she in a position to do so, Barbara would be the first to tell me to remarry.'

'You were out with another woman when she killed herself.'

'Yes, I was. And have I thanked my lucky stars over that!'

Despite all the years she had known him, this still shocked her. 'You . . . you rotten swine!'

He raised an eyebrow. 'You sounded quite vicious then . . . Obviously, you've never stopped to realize that if I'd been in Middle Manor when Babs killed herself, I'd have had absolutely no alibi. Can you imagine what those knuckle-headed detectives would have thought then? . . . No, Sandra did me a good turn.'

'If you don't stop seeing Rosalie I'll tell her what really happened and how you were out with that woman.'

He shrugged his shoulders. 'I can't stop you, of course, but I do warn you that she won't believe you.'

'Yes, she will. It's the truth.'

'The truth so often sounds highly unbelievable . . . Perhaps I ought to add that it's only a couple of days since we were talking about you and she was saying how she was becoming fed up with having you hang round her so much.'

She gasped. 'Rosalie wouldn't ever have said that about me.'

'Naturally, I tried to explain. I said that when you were

emotionally involved you tended not to see things straight and that's why, although I've never given you the slightest cause—only a cad tells all—you were terribly jealous of her.'

'You . . . you said that?'

'So now I'm afraid that whatever you say will be disbelieved and put down to that little green-eyed goddess. Why goddess incidentally? I'd have thought dæmon queen was far more apposite.'

She knew a bitter sense of humiliation.

His tone became mocking. 'You really ought to learn not to move out of your class, Gertie . . . Now, sit down and let me get you a drink and we'll declare all bygones to be bygones.'

She swallowed heavily. 'I'll tell the English police. I'll tell those detectives that you weren't in my house when Barbara died.'

He came to his feet.

'I won't see Rosalie's life being ruined. If you don't leave her alone, I'll fly back and tell them what really happened. That you weren't with me, you were out with Sandra. And that you were very close to Middle Manor.'

He came forward and as he did so he ran his fingertips around his scarred cheek. 'You won't tell them anything.'

'You can't keep me quiet like that.'

He suddenly hit her across the side of her face, knocking her backwards. She tripped over the arm of a chair and collapsed on to the seat. And then, shocked and frightened by the physical violence, her memory suddenly returned to the day when his cheek had become scarred. And for the first time since then she remembered everything. He'd jeered at her and, frightened he'd refuse to be friends any more, she'd got the key from the kitchen. She'd unlocked the door of the room and he'd pushed past her. He'd looked around and when he'd seen the almost bare table and shelves, covered in dust, he'd contemptuously told her that there was nothing there that was going to make her father's fortune. Then he'd noticed an earthenware bowl on the top shelf and he'd demanded to know what was in it? She'd had no idea and had said that whatever it was, it was probably dangerous. He'd jeered at her again. And *he* had moved a chair and climbed on to it, *he* had picked up the earthenware bowl, *he* had tripped and in tripping had splashed his cheek with acid . . .

Now, mental pain was added to the physical pain of that blow. The lies had caused her agonies of guilt when young and he had deliberately, callously let her suffer. He was far, far more rotten than she had ever suspected. So rotten that he had made use of her whenever he needed help, scorned her when didn't. Those months in her flat had not been spent with a man who, even if only temporarily, was in love with her: they had been spent with a man who had said he was in love but who had used her because he'd nowhere else to go . . .

His harsh voice interrupted her bitter thoughts. 'I'll kill you before you get the chance to do anything like that.'

CHAPTER 10

The office was very hot, despite the fact that the window was wide open, the shutters were closed, and the fan on the desk was turned to its higher speed. Alvarez found such difficulty in keeping his eyelids open that in the end, and with a sigh of contentment, he no longer bothered as he slumped deeper into the chair. His thoughts drifted away into the inconsequential chaos which immediately preceded sleep.

The telephone rang. He slowly, reluctantly reached out for the receiver, swearing as he did so.

'Is that Inspector Alvarez?' asked the woman with a plum in her mouth.

'Yes,' he answered sadly.

'I have Superior Chief Salas on the line for you.'

There was a pause. He closed his eyes once more: almost certainly, Salas was not held up on business, he was biding his time in order to underline his authority.

'Are you there?'

The rasping words caused him to start heavily. 'Indeed, señor.'

'Do you remember Señorita Dean?'

He racked his brain, trying to place the person.

'For God's sake, man, you interviewed her in Caraitx.'

The mention of Caraitx identified her. 'Yes, of course, señor. It was just that for a moment I . . .'

'She's been found dead, in circumstances which make it quite clear she committed suicide. Take charge of the matter.'

'Señor, Caraitx is not within my area and although I did, of course, interview her in the past, this was only because Inspector Antignac was unusually busy at the time . . .'

'He's still extremely busy.'

'I've also got an exceptional workload . . .'

'I wouldn't doubt for one moment that you should have,' said Salas nastily. 'However, in case you have forgotten, Inspector Antignac does not speak English and you do and so you will conduct the enquiry. Remember one thing. On no account are you to complicate the issue, as you have unfortunately done in the past.'

'It's never been me who's complicated anything, but the facts . . .' He stopped when he realized the connection had been cut. He sighed, replaced the receiver. 'To the devil with the English!' he said aloud. He leaned over, opened the bottom right-hand drawer of his desk, and brought out a bottle of brandy and a tumbler. He poured himself out a very generous drink. There were times when a man needed comforting.

The ancient, squeaking Seat 600 dragged itself up Calle Padre Vives, finally coming to a jerky halt in front of No. 15. Alvarez crossed the narrow pavement, found the front door unlocked, and stepped inside.

'Who's that?' demanded a man.

'The governor-general.'

A squat, ugly, cheerful policeman, dressed in the summer uniform of the municipal police — white shirt and dark blue trousers — came out of the kitchen to stand in the arched doorway. 'Are you the inspector from Llueso they said was coming?'

They studied each other with instinctive reservation. It was a well-known fact in Llueso that everyone from Caraitx was a rogue: it was a well-known fact in Caraitx that everyone from Llueso was untrustworthy.

The policeman jerked his head towards the ceiling. 'She's upstairs, in the bedroom.'

'D'you know who found her?'

'The woman who comes and does here, a few mornings a week.'

'Where's she now?'

'Gone back to her own place. Wasn't any use her hanging on here, was it?'

'Has the doctor been?'

'Yeah. And he said to tell you that he couldn't wait around. The best thing for you to do is have a word with him later on at his place: that is, if you want to.'

'I expect I'll want a word with both of 'em.'

'Suit yourself.'

The stairs, which had a half turn in the middle, led to a passage/landing off which were four doors. The only closed door gave access to the dead woman's bedroom.

The shutters were closed, but the curtains were drawn

and there was sufficient light entering between the louvres for him to see the bed in rough detail. Gertrude, wearing pyjamas, lay without any bedclothes over her. Her head was encased in a large plastic bag. He crossed himself. Death was the final mystery and whatever the state of one's faith, it was only prudent to respect it.

As he went towards the window, his right foot kicked something small which skidded across the tiled floor. It was impossible to identify what that something was. He opened the shutters and clipped them back and the fierce sunlight shafted into the room. He turned and looked down to find out what he'd kicked and saw, in the middle of the floor, several pieces of what looked to have been an earthenware cazuela, or cooking pot: one of the pieces was now several feet from the rest.

He crossed to the bed. Her eyes were shut and there was a twist to her mouth, rather as if she'd been ironically amused about something just before she'd died. To the right of the bed was a small table with a single drawer, and on this were two paperbacks, a box of tissues, a half full medicine bottle and, propped up against the bottle, a typewritten note on a sheet of headed notepaper.

I've had the pain for a long time, but recently it's been getting much worse. Pat's sister wrote last week to say that Pat had died from cancer after months of agony because the doctors wouldn't give her enough pain-killers. I can't face going through that. I'm just not brave enough.

He replaced the note. The wording suggested she hadn't consulted a doctor, so it was possible that in fact she hadn't been suffering from cancer after all. But her fears had grown and grown until they'd overwhelmed her . . .

Next to her bedroom was a studio. Three unframed

canvases were leaning against a wall and a fourth one was
on a large easel: paints, palettes, palette knives, bottles of
unidentified liquids, brushes, stained rags, and paint-
boxes, were strewn haphazardly almost everywhere. He
briefly studied the three canvases against the wall and
found them conventionally attractive: the kind of
paintings he wouldn't have minded on the walls at home.
He moved and looked at the fourth, and unfinished, one
on the easel. A background of mountains, a distant finca
with grey walls and roof of Roman tiles, a drystone wall,
almond trees, and in the left foreground a gnarled,
twisted olive tree whose trunk, largely hollow, was metres
in circumference so that the branches growing from it
seemed disproportionate . . . It was only as he left and was
stepping into the passage that it occurred to him there'd
been some quality to that unfinished painting which was
disturbing.

The third room was a spare bedroom, the fourth and
last a bathroom. He returned downstairs.

'Who's got the front-door key?'

'I have,' replied the municipal policeman.

'You can hang on to it, then. You'll have to let the
undertakers in. And in the meantime, you can show me
where the doctor and the daily woman live.'

'I've a mountain of work waiting at the station.'

'That's just going to have to wait, isn't it?' Alvarez was
pleased to be able to upset someone else's morning.

Señora Garcia's face was tanned and heavily lined,
witness to all the hours spent out in the fields under the
grilling sun when younger. She was garrulous and
possessed a natural liking for histrionics.

'I knew there was something wrong the moment I
entered the house. I knew it.'

Alvarez, sitting at the kitchen table, nodded, his
round, stolid face showing no signs of impatience.

She returned to chopping an onion. 'You see, it was all so quiet. Like a tomb. Usually, the señorita had the radio or a record-player on. A great one for music, she was: and some of it was strange, I can tell you.' She upended the knife and used the blunt edge to sweep the chopped onion into a cooking pot. 'I shouted out, "Señorita, it's me. I've brought you an empanada." She loved my empanadas . . .' Quite suddenly, the tears were rolling down her cheeks. 'She was so kind and nice. To think she could kill herself. Sweet Holy Mother!' She dried her eyes with the edge of her apron, reached across for a couple of carrots, and peeled them. Life was full of sorrow, but there was never much time for grieving.

'D'you think she'd been depressed recently?'

'Something was wrong: I know that much. When she first came to the village, she was sad, but soon . . .' She stared down at the chopping-board as she tried to find the words to express what she wanted to say. 'She smiled and talked to everyone and made friends. She came into our homes for merienda. But just recently, she'd not been smiling any more. I said to her, "Señorita, are you ill? Has something terrible happened?" But she never told me what the trouble was.'

'When did she first become depressed?'

She thought, her face screwed up in concentration, as she chopped the peeled carrots. 'I suppose it was about when Ines started teething.'

'And when did Ines start teething?'

'Somewhere around the end of last month,' she answered vaguely.

Dr Méndez lived on the outskirts of the village, at a point where the hill had begun to level out so that the land dropped only gently. The house was faced with rock, not limestone blocks, and it stood in its own grounds, one of only a few to do so.

Méndez's face was thin and his expression harassed. His wife, who let Alvarez into the house, was considerably younger than he, was dressed very smartly, and wore a considerable amount of jewellery. The doctor's harassment, decided Alvarez, was emotional rather than professional.

The sitting-room faced south and, despite the fact the house was near the foot of the hill, offered much the same dramatic view across the central plain to mountains and sea as was visible from higher up. Méndez, once Alvarez was seated, began to pace the floor, deftly rounding a small table on which were three pieces of Lladro ware. 'I was called to the house at roughly nine-thirty. By then, she'd been dead for quite some time.' He rushed the words and clipped the sentences short, as if very pressed for time.

'Roughly, when did she die?'

His tone became impatient. 'Not much point, surely, when it's so obviously suicide? But if you must have a figure, call it twelve hours.'

'And she died from asphyxiation?'

He came to a sudden stop. 'Yes. Will you be calling for a PM?'

'I doubt it. I take it you read the suicide note?'

'Yes, I did.'

Alvarez said slowly: 'It's sad to think of someone committing suicide without ever finding out if her fears were justified.'

'It happens,' said the doctor grimly.

Back in his over-hot, stuffy office, Alvarez telephoned Palma. He was very grateful to hear that Superior Chief Salas was out and he made his report to the woman with a plum in her mouth. The English señorita had committed suicide by pulling a plastic bag over her head, probably after taking some sleeping pills. Everything appeared to be straightforward and therefore there seemed to be no point in asking for a PM. However, in case the superior chief decided that as a foreigner was involved a PM was justified, the body would be held at the mortuary for forty-eight hours before arrangements were put in hand for the funeral.

CHAPTER 11

The intermittent noise broke through Alvarez's sleep and scattered his dreams, but when it ceased he thankfully began once more to drift away . . .

'It's the station,' Dolores shouted from downstairs.

He opened his eyes and stared up at the ceiling of his bedroom, very dimly seen in the light which filtered through both shutters and curtains.

'Are you coming down, then?'

He slowly manœuvred himself into a sitting position.

'Are you dead up there?'

No such luck. He dressed in shirt and trousers and, bare-footed, made his way downstairs.

Dolores, as coolly handsome as a flamenco queen, said: 'You look terrible.'

'If you knew how I felt! . . . What lunatic at the station is ringing up this early in the afternoon?'

'It's only early to someone who's drunk a bottle of coñac and been snoring like a matanza pig.'

Before all that nonsense about women's lib, he thought sourly, a woman had known her place and stuck to it. He crossed to the telephone. 'Yeah?'

'Been on holiday, have you? . . . You're handling the suicide case in Caraitx, aren't you?'

'What if I am?'

'There's an Englishman been ringing up and creating.

Inspector Antignac says you're to see him and find out what in the hell he's on about.'

'The case is closed.'

'You argue that out with the inspector. And in case you're interested, the Englishman lives at Ca'n Noyeta.'

'Where's that?'

'Near Caraitx.'

'How near?'

'How would I know?'

Alvarez replaced the receiver and walked into the kitchen where Dolores was beginning to prepare the supper. He slumped down into a handy chair. 'I wouldn't say no to a coffee.'

She picked up the kettle, filled it from the cold tap, and placed it on the gas stove. The gas refused to light. 'The bottle must need changing.'

In the old days, he thought, no woman would have dreamed of asking a man to do a household chore. Reluctantly, he dragged himself to his feet and went through the small enclosed patio to the passageway in which they kept the gas bottles.

Around Caraitx, the land was light grey in colour, very stony, and poor in heart. Almonds and algarrobas grew freely, but only where there was irrigation and there had been heavy fertilizing with dung or well-weathered seaweed was it possible to grow the kind of crops seen everywhere around Llueso. But there was one crop, which grew without the need of any irrigation, for which the district was justly famous: the Caraitx melon. How they grew, when they were never watered and no rain fell for weeks on end, was a miracle. And since any miracle needed to be celebrated and propitiated, on the first Saturday of every June a special service of thanksgiving was held in Caraitx church, when farmers gave thanks for miracles past and — although this was never actually stated aloud—pleaded for miracles to come. When the small, very dark green melons, white veined, were harvested, any man could join the gods and dine on ambrosia and nectar.

When Alvarez came abreast of the first of the melon fields, he slowed the car and stared at the rows of plants, as yet bearing only small, rock-hard fruit, and as he conjured up the icy sweetness of the mature melon, he cursed the Englishman who was responsible for his having to be on the road when the heat was so stifling. He cursed the Englishman much harder when, twenty-three minutes later, a third set of direction to Ca'n Noyeta proved to be wrong.

With considerable difficulty, he turned the car and bounced his way back along the dirt track to the metalled road. A mule cart, with squealing axle, driven by a man who was slumped in half sleep, came along. He shouted through the opened car window: 'D'you know where Ca'n Noyeta is?'

The cart stopped. The driver remained slumped, his face hidden by a wide-brimmed raffia hat.

'Where's Ca'n Noyeta?' Alvarez shouted still louder.

The man slowly lifted his head until his heavily stubbled chin and toothless mouth became visible. He considered the question for a long time before saying: 'Is that the house of the Englishman who . . .'

'Who what?'

The man hawked and spat. 'Up the road, first track on the left and keep going until you see the house of the Englishman who . . .'

'In the name of the devil, who what?'

The man grinned: it was the grin of a satyr. Then he shouted at the mule to continue and lowered his head.

The dirt track wandered through the countryside: a hundred years previously, a traveller would have seen exactly the same scene as now. That Caraitx bastard, thought Alvarez, sending him into the blue for a laugh . . .

Finally, after a sharp left-hand bend, a house came in sight. Initially, he was certain that this couldn't be Ca'n Noyeta: in a bad state of repair, without electricity, telephone, garden, or swimming pool, it was inconceivable that an Englishman could be living in it. Yet as he drew nearer, he saw a nameboard which, in very artistic lettering, identified it as the house he sought.

He parked behind a Renault 6 which looked as if it had escaped from a breaker's yard. He crossed to the front door, knocked, and after a while heard a woman's footsteps approaching. He pictured a dispirited, middle-aged wife who with her husband had come to the island when the cost of living was so much less and it had been possible to enjoy life on a small income . . .

Liza opened the door. She was wearing a bikini, but only just. He realized he was gawking at her, but it was not often one actually met the centrefold from *Playboy*.

'What do you want?' she asked in thickly accented Spanish.

He pulled himself together. 'I am from the Cuerpo General de Policía, señora,' he replied, in English. 'Is your husband inside?'

She giggled. 'I sure hope not! The last time I heard anything about him, he was in Manchester . . . You mean Bruno. Sure, he's in. Come on through.'

As he followed her through the house, he tried not to concentrate on the delightful way in which her largely visible buttocks moved as she walked.

Bruno and Norah were sunbathing on rugs set out on the ground at the back of the house. He was wearing very brief trunks, she the botton half of a bikini that somehow managed to be even briefer. They sat up. Norah flashed Alvarez a dazzling smile, said 'Hi!', picked up a glass and drained it. Only then, as an afterthought, did she bother to find the top half of the bikini and slip this on.

Alvarez said, with great formality. 'Good afternoon, Señora Meade.'

Norah giggled. 'Grab that, Bruno! Señora Meade!'

It was obvious that she was not Señora Meade. Alvarez began to feel as if he were caught up in an erotic dream. 'Señor, I understand you've been speaking to the police in Caraitx about the death of Señorita Dean?'

Bruno came to his feet with athletic ease. He scratched his bronzed, hairy chest. 'I don't give a bugger what anyone says, the old girl didn't commit suicide.'

'Señor, I was in the house of the unfortunate señorita this morning and all the evidence suggests that she did tragically kill herself.'

'Stuff the evidence . . . Here, let's go on inside and find something to drink.'

In the sitting-room, Alvarez sat on one of the decrepit armchairs, apprehensive that it might collapse under him. He stared at the paintings on the walls and wondered what, if anything, they were meant to represent.

Liza came into the room with a battered *papier-mâché* tray on which were glass tumblers, a bowl of ice cubes, and a bottle half full of brandy: she put the tray down on the wooden box that did duty as a table. Meade emptied the bottle into the tumblers and Liza added as many ice cubes as each glass would then hold.

'Why are you so damned knuckle-headed as to think Gertie killed herself?' Meade demanded, as he handed Alvarez one of the tumblers.

'Apart from any other reason, señor, because she left a note in which she said she was going to commit suicide.'

He looked surprised. 'So did it say anything else: like why?'

'She feared she had cancer and had just heard that a friend of hers in England had died from that disease after many months of pain. She could not face the future.'

'I just don't believe all that.'

'I myself read the note . . .'

'I'm saying I don't believe she thought she had cancer. We used to talk about everything and if she'd thought that, she'd have told us.'

'It is a subject people often do not like to discuss.'

'If she'd been worried, she'd have told us.' He turned to face Norah. 'Isn't that right?'

'I think so,' she replied. 'After all, we were her friends.'

'Yeah.' Meade looked back at Alvarez. 'D'you know something? Before she came out here, she hardly knew anyone: to talk to as friends, I mean. So with us she talked all the time about anything. She'd have shared her fears if she had any.'

'She'd have known we'd have done everything we could to help,' agreed Liza.

'Señor, I am sure that from your point of view what you say is correct, but how correct is your point of view?' Alvarez thought for a few seconds. 'Even from friends of many years, people keep secrets. If the señorita had told you her fears, would you not have insisted she see a doctor? And that might have been to confirm her very worst fears . . . Do you understand what I am trying to say?'

'Of course. But it's all a load of cod's. One thing. Who is this friend who's just died? Gertie told us often enough she hadn't a single real friend back home.'

'I know only that her name was Pat.'

'She's never mentioned anyone called Pat . . . And if she was all that frightened about herself, how come she was here on Sunday night, laughing her head off and planning an exhibition?'

'This last Sunday?'

'That's what I just said.'

'Did she perhaps not seem to be just a little upset over something?'

'She was upset over nothing. She even had a few more drinks than usual and we bloody near had her doing "Knees Up, Mother Brown".'

'You mentioned an exhibition—was this to be of her paintings?'

'Only a small one. And it was to be in Llueso because there's a whole raft of painters live there: leastwise, that's what the bloody ignoramuses call themselves. She only painted commercially, of course.'

'Bruno paints,' said Norah, with tremendous pride.

'Artistically,' said Liza, to make the point quite clear.

Alvarez looked up at a couple of the paintings opposite where he sat and tried to seem intelligently appreciative.

'Funny thing is, I reckon that if she'd learned to spit on the money, she could've become a proper painter.' Meade sounded as if this were not an admission which came easily. 'When I saw that last picture of hers, I told her straight, for me that's not chocolate box, that's art . . . D'you see it?'

'There was an unfinished painting on the easel.'

'What was the composition?'

'An olive tree, an almond orchard, a finca, and mountains.'

'Original,' sneered Meade. Then his tone altered. 'But the way she'd nailed that olive tree! You just knew it was a thousand years old, that it had stared, caring but impotent, at all the stupidities and tragedies of life . . .'

Alvarez remembered how, after first seeing it, he had briefly sensed something chilling, even macabre about that painting. 'Perhaps, señor, it was expressing the fears of a woman who believed she had a fatal cancer?'

Meade was clearly surprised by a possibility which had not occurred to him. He drained his glass, fiddled with it to spin the half-melted cubes around the edge, then said:

'Get another bottle, Liza.'

'There's nothing more of anything, not even vino,' she answered.

'Jeeze! Who goddamn well keeps drinking all the booze?'

'Do you know when the señorita came to live on this island?' Alvarez asked.

Meade shrugged his shoulders, his mind troubled by the lack of alcohol.

'Must be quite a long time now,' said Norah vaguely.

'And has she made many friends?'

'Gertie got on well with almost all the villagers. But maybe you're talking about the Brits? There was us, of course. And Rosalie. And Angus and Maude who live a couple of kilometres from here, but Angus can't stop nipping bums and Gertie wasn't very fond of that. And then there's George and Joan . . .'

'She couldn't stand the sight of 'em,' said Meade roughly. 'Which is hardly to be wondered at.'

Norah giggled, 'You don't like George because he said your paintings reminded him of the ones that chimpanzee did.'

'Ignorant old fool.' Meade drank the melted ice in his glass, hoping it might contain a faint flavour of brandy.

'You've forgotten Keir West,' said Liz.

'That bloody scripe? She'd too much taste to be friendly with him, even if she did know him back in England.'

Alvarez drove up the tortuous streets of Caraitx and parked at the top end of Calle Padre Vives. Bruno Meade was a roistering, amoral braggart (to think of him in such terms might help to stifle envy of his life style) so how did this affect the value of his evidence? He was quite certain the señorita could not have committed suicide—yet the circumstances of her death were fully consistent with suicide. And if her death had not been suicide, then it must have been murder and not even he had been able to suggest the slightest motive for murder . . .

Meade had made only two really valid points. In the past, the señorita had never once expressed the slightest fear about her health and on the Sunday she had been lively and cheerful and full of plans for a forthcoming exhibition. But wasn't that brightness likely to have been the brittle nerve-stretched brightness of someone who knew that soon it would all be over . . . ?

He sighed. All too clearly, he was now going to have to make more enquiries before he could safely wrap up the case and forget it.

He left the car and walked along the pavement to No. 14, stepped inside the doorway and called out. A woman in her early fifties, dressed in the black which until recently had been worn by all widows no matter how long their husbands had been dead, came into the entrance room which was also the formal sitting-room. He introduced himself. Initially, she was flustered, believing his visit must mean trouble, but he reassured her and explained that he merely wanted to ask a few questions concerning the señorita next door.

'The poor woman,' she said, once seated. 'To think she was so'frightened that she killed herself . . .' She shook her head, unable to comprehend how anyone could be so devoid of faith as to be unable to face what lay ahead in life.

He asked her how well she had known Gertrude.

'She'd come in here quite often and have a bowl of soup or some cocoa with an ensaimada an we'd talk. I'd visit her house. We were good friends and neighbours.'

'Would you describe her as a happy woman?'

'Señor, what is a happy woman?'

It was a simple question, but far too profound for him to try to answer. 'Did she talk a lot about her health?'

'Her health? I don't think she ever mentioned it. Most

of all, she wanted to know about the village and our customs: she'd ask why we did this or that and I wouldn't know. As I said, it's just what we've always done . . . And then sometimes she'd talk just a little about her painting and show me what she'd done. She was a really wonderful painter.'

He nodded. 'Did she have many foreign visitors?'

'No, not many. A man with a beard, who always talks very loudly: he has two . . . friends. A woman who is very nice and she speaks French to me and I speak Mallorquin back and sometimes we manage to understand each other a little.'

'Did anyone come to see her on Monday night?'

'There was no one before I went to bed, but I went early as I so often do because I get tired at work and then come back and have to cook the evening meal and Emilio always likes a big one, even in the heat.'

'What time d'you reckon it was when you went to bed?'

'Perhaps about nine.'

'And you wouldn't know if anyone called next door after that?'

'No, that I wouldn't. But Emilio may have heard if anyone did because his room overlooks the road.'

'I take it, he's your son?'

She answered with great pride. Emilio was just like her beloved husband—who had died almost twelve years ago in an accident at the quarry—and now he was in his last year at the Institute, doing BUP, the next year he would go on to do COU, and after that, God willing, he would be at university, unless he did his military service first. And this would be a miracle because no member of the family had ever before been to a university except for her uncle who had once worked at Salamanca University as a porter.

'Is he at home, señora, so I could have a word with him?'

'He's up in his room, working at his books.'

Emilio was dressed in a T-shirt and jeans: across the front of the T-shirt was printed in English, 'My two are bigger'.

'This señor is from the police,' his mother told him.

He assumed an air of sullen innocence.

'He wants to know about any visitors the English señorita had on Monday night. Your room looks on to the road, doesn't it?'

'Of course it does,' he answered contemptuously.

Alvarez said: 'What time did you work up to on Monday?'

'Ten, same as always.'

'Did you hear anyone call next door?'

'I wasn't listening, was I, if I was working.'

'Did you hear any cars drive up the road?'

'Cars are always coming up to turn.'

'Did one stop outside the señorita's house?'

'Never heard one.'

'Are you quite sure?' asked his mother, nervously eager to help Alvarez.

'Haven't I said?'

If it would not have distressed his mother too much, Alvarez would have taught him some manners.

CHAPTER 12

Juan stepped into Alvarez's bedroom. 'Mummy says to tell you that you're late and if you don't hurry up there'll be no cocoa.'

Alvarez opened his eyes. 'No cocoa?'

'Isabel and me will drink it all.'

'Do that and I'll clap you both in jail . . . Why aren't you at school?'

'Because it's the fiesta of schools. I told you it was going to be, yesterday evening.'

'I'm afraid I'd forgotten.'

'You're getting very old,' said Juan, before he went out and closed the door behind him.

Alvarez climbed out of bed, crossed to the small mirror on the dresser, and looked at himself. A little tired, perhaps — and small wonder, with his workload — but certainly not very old . . .

Downstairs, in the kitchen, as bright-eyed as ever, Dolores was slicing carrots. 'Sometimes I wonder you don't take root in bed.'

'Perhaps because I'm never given the chance,' he answered lugubriously.

She smiled. 'Sit down and I'll make you some cocoa. Juan's been out to get you a croissant to go with it.'

'In that case, I'll forgive him.'

'For what?'

'For suggesting that I'm getting very old.'

'To a youngster like him, we're all as old as the hills.'

He sat at the table. 'D'you think being educated will change him?'

'What nonsense is that?'

He told her about Emilio.

'It's the mother's fault,' she said immediately.

'A widow, an only son . . . It's very difficult.'

'Not if you teach them from the beginning how to behave.'

It was never really that simple, he thought. Emilio's mother, early left a widow, would have done everything possible for him. Yet her love had bred resentment instead of gratitude. He sighed heavily.

'Now what's the matter?'

'I was thinking how unjust the world can be.'

'If that's all you've got to worry about, you're lucky. And if you've nothing better to do, you might get the milk from the fridge.'

He left the house half an hour later, sat behind the wheel of his car, and wondered whether to go to his office before driving on to Caraitx? The thought that urgent work might have come in and be awaiting his immediate attention decided him. He drove off in the direction of Caraitx.

In No. 15, Calle Padre Vives, the body was no longer on the bed, but otherwise the main bedroom was exactly as he had last seen it. He studied the clothes she had worn on the last day and which when she had undressed had been carelessly thrown down on the seat of a chair and he went over and carefully folded them up. That done, he began to search the room. The bed had on it only two pillows, two sheets, and a bedspread. He stripped everything, examined the mattress, folded up the sheets and blankets and placed them on the mattress and coverd them with the bedspread. He checked the things on top of the bedside table, opened the medicine bottle and rolled a couple of the capsules on to the palm of his left hand, after which he returned them and replaced the cap. He opened the single drawer in the table and looked through the clutter of personal items.

A built-in cupboard ran the length of one wall and as he crossed towards this his right foot crunched down on one of the pieces of broken earthenware. He bent down and collected them all up: as far as it was possible to tell, the cazuela had been clean when it had broken. He put the pieces down on one end of the dressing-table.

The cupboard was divided vertically into four compartments, two of which contained drawers or open shelving. In the left-hand compartment hung the few dresses, skirts, slacks, and coats, of a woman who could seldom be bothered with her appearance: in a rack on the floor were half a dozen pairs of shoes, all serviceable rather than fashionable. In the next compartment, shelved, were tights, belts, blouses, underclothes, and sweaters. The third compartment contained two drawers and open shelving and some of the shelves had been used to store papers, most of which were in obvious disorder. In the fourth and final compartment were several empty cardboard boxes, two heavily patched, paint-stained smocks, and a portable typewriter in its case. He returned to the papers. There were files, loose letters, letters still in their envelopes, bank statements, cheque-stubs, and handwritten notes. One file dealt with investments. It soon became clear that she had been reasonably well off, but not wealthy. In another file was her will in Spanish, an English translation of this, and some handwritten notes. He read the Spanish will, dated several months previously. In view of her long-standing debt, she left everything she owned to Keir West. He scratched the back of his neck. That was a name he'd surely met before . . . It was the death of West's wife which had led to the señorita being questioned: Meade had referred to West in scathing terms . . . He finished reading the will and turned to the notes. She had intended to alter her will and leave everything to Rosalie Rassaud—another name Meade had mentioned? Or had it been one of those beautiful, long-legged, proud-busted . . . It seemed as if no new will had ever been executed. There were cheque-books on the National Westminster in Petercross and the Banco de Credito Balear in Inca and several books of stubs for both those banks. The stubs suggested that the Mallorquin bank had been used to meet the day-to-day costs of living and the English bank only when it became necessary to pay into the Mallorquin bank a sterling cheque for immediate credit of pesetas. In a third folder there was a jumble of receipts which dated from recently to the day when she'd first moved into the house. He quickly flipped through them: Seat 600, various servicings and repairs to this, canvases, paints, and brushes, again and again, a large number of framings, an electric toaster some nine months previously, a record-player and a number of records a month after that, typewriter a fortnight before, a food mixer only four days previously . . . Sad mementoes of a life in a foreign land which had been built up slowly, destroyed abruptly. He fiddled with the receipt for the food mixer. Would a woman, contemplating suicide as she must have been four days ago, have bothered to buy a food mixer? After a while, he dismissed the question. A person contemplating suicide was in a state of mental confusion and could hardly be judged by logical standards.

Overcoming his natural dislike of prying too deeply into someone else's private life, he looked through the relatively few personal letters. These dated back through several months and without exception were couched in terms of acquaintanceship rather than friendship. He failed to find the letter from Pat's sister which, according to the suicide note, had finally triggered off her suicide. Since she kept other letters, why had she not kept this one? Did its absence suggest there had never been such a letter? Much more likely that she had read it and then torn it up, impotently trying to dismiss the sad news—in the old days, the bearer of bad news was often executed.

He left the bedroom and went next door, into the studio, where he stood in front of the easel and studied the olive tree in the unfinished painting. Meade had been right. The tree had been executed with a power that simply was not present in the other three paintings. Surely something quite extraordinary must have happened to sharpen her artistic talents to such a degree? A fear, growing slowly, perhaps even subconsciously, suddenly accelerated when it was exposed by the letter from Pat's sister?

The spare bedroom and the bathroom provided nothing of interest and he went downstairs and searched the sitting-room, wash-house, and small cloakroom. Moving on to the kitchen, he looked for plastic bags and found several, in two different sizes, neither of which was the same as that of the bag which had been over the dead woman's head . . . If a person were contemplating suicide by use of a bag, wouldn't she obtain two or three of the right size just in case something initially went wrong? Logically, yes. But he'd already decided she could not have been in a logical frame of mind.

He returned to the sitting-room and stood in the centre. He'd uncovered one or two facts (if they were facts?) which did raise questions, but this could well be only because he had been conditioned to look for trouble. What did he know for certain? . . . Did he now accept that the evidence was straightforward and so dismiss Meade's allegations as nonsense, or did he concentrate on possible queries and follow these up as far as possible in order to make certain there was not any real significance in them? Reluctantly, he realized that he really must follow them up . . .

Rigo, a solicitor, lived and worked in a large, rambling house, built around a square patio in which there was a very ornate fountain. His offices consisted of two rooms, the first both a waiting-room and where his clerk worked, amid a clutter of books, files, and papers, the second where he worked, in some considerable style. He was short, had bushy hair, a jaunty face, and the friendly and open manner of a born diplomat or confidence trickster.

'There are one or two points in connection with the señorita's death which have to be tidied up,' said Alvarez, as he sat in front of the large and expensively inlaid and leathered desk. 'I've come across a copy of her will.' He passed it across. 'Did you draw it up?'

Rigo briefly checked it. 'Yes, I did.'

'Any idea what she's worth?'

'None whatsoever. I remember she told me she'd investments in England, but she named no figures.'

'Did she own the house she was living in, in Padre Vives?'

'No. She rented it on an eleven month lease.'

'Did you know she was intending to alter her will?'

'She called in not very long ago and asked me how one went about altering a will in Spain. I explained it was sufficient to make a new one and have it registered in Madrid, but naturally it was much better if one specifically abrogated the earlier one.'

'Did she consult you about drawing up a new will?'

'No, she didn't.'

'Did she ever give you any indication of what sort of a relationship existed between herself and Señor West?'

'West?' Rigo frowned.

'She's the man to whom she left everything in the will you've got there.'

'Of course! I'm afraid I didn't read it right through just now and I've forgotten the details . . . No, beyond naming him as the sole beneficiary, I can't remember her as saying anything about him.'

Alvarez hesitated, then stood. 'Thanks for all your help.'

'Is there some sort of trouble concerning West?'

'At the moment, I just wouldn't know.'

Rigo, to whom the devious way was always to be preferred, accepted that as a tactical prevarication. He smiled his appreciation, showing three gold teeth.

As the car rounded the left-hand turn in the dirt track, Ca'n Absel came into view above the orange trees. Money, Alvarez immediately thought. To buy or rent a large house like this in the Huerta, where it enjoyed privacy yet was under a kilometre from the village, called for a great deal of money. He could remember when the whole of the Huerta had been devoted to farming, as it should have been according to its name, and it had not been a haven for the rich foreigners who caused the good, rich soil to be overlaid with their gilded homes.

He parked by the lean-to garage in which were a Mercedes and a Seat. He walked along the tiled patio, under the vines with their dozens of bunches of as-yet undeveloped grapes, and knocked on the front door. Francisca and he recognized each other on sight. 'Francisca!' he said warmly. 'How's Lucía? I heard she had to go into Palma for an operation?'

'She did. But I went to the clinic the day before yesterday and saw her and she's had the operation and says she hasn't felt so well in ages.'

'What good news! Dolores will be delighted to hear it. Give Lucía our very best wishes.'

'Of course.'

'Is the señor in?'

'Sure. D'you want a word with him? Come in and I'll tell him.'

She showed him into the sitting-room and left. Surrounded by luxurious furniture, cosseted by air-conditioning, looking out across a large swimming pool at the rich countryside, he decided that the old saw that money couldn't buy everything must have been coined by the wealthy.

West came through the inside doorway. 'Good morning, señor,' Alvarez said, briefly wondering what could have caused the scarring on the cheek. 'I must apologize for troubling you.'

'No trouble at all, just provided I can leave here in an hour's time when I've an appointment,' West replied easily. 'Now, first things first, what can I get you to drink?'

'Might I have a brandy, please?'

'With soda and ice?'

'Just ice, thank you.'

West crossed to a mobile cocktail cabinet, opened out the top flaps which automatically brought up a rack containing bottles and glasses, and poured out a brandy for Alvarez and a whisky for himself.

Alvarez drank, then said: 'I expect you have heard the sad news of Señorita Dean's death?'

West nodded. 'Came as one hell of a shock. In fact, when Tom told me, I wouldn't believe it . . . Thing is, we'd been friends since we were kids together, so suddenly to be told she'd killed herself . . . I suppose that is true—she did commit suicide?'

'I am afraid that it certainly appears to be so.'

'To think she'd become so desperate . . .'

His concern seemed genuine. 'Señor, I am here, now, to try to understand a little more about the señorita.'

'I take it there'll have to be an inquest, or whatever the local equivalent is, and you'll need evidence about her mental state?'

'There will probably be that, yes. But my immediate reason for asking questions is because it has been suggested that the señorita did not, in fact, kill herself.'

'Not? You've just said that she did.'

'I believe I said that it appears she did. The circumstances surrounding the señorita's death all suggest suicide, but a friend of hers, an Englishman, has said that it is quite impossible that she would ever have killed herself.'

'He's saying it was an accident, then?'

'It could not have been an accident. The señorita had a plastic bag over her head: there was a note.'

'But if it wasn't suicide and couldn't have been an accident . . . Are you claiming it was . . .' He stopped.

'Murder, señor.'

'For God's sake, who'd want to murder Gertie?'

'I cannot answer. That is what I have to try to discover.'

'Who's this Englishman who's been shouting the odds?'
'Señor Meade.'
'Him? He's nothing but a beachcomber.'
'Perhaps. But he was a friend of the señorita's.'
'And I'll tell you why! He hasn't two pesetas to rub together and so he made up to her so she'd supply him and those two tarts of his with booze . . . You can forget anything and everything he's said.'
'He was quite certain that the señorita was not in any way depressed just before she died.'
'How would he know one way or the other?'
'She was at his house on the Sunday.'
'So what does that signify, when he'll have been too tight to judge whether she was laughing or crying. He doesn't know any more about Gertie's mental state than . . .' He stopped, hesitated, then said, far more calmly: 'I'm sorry, I'm shouting my head off. But it was one hell of a shock to hear you say she could have been murdered and then to discover you were going on something Meade had told you . . . The real truth is, Gertie's always been mentally unstable: ever since she was a kid. You just never knew how to take her. She'd be laughing one moment and crying the next: she'd get in a rage over nothing and after calming down would indulge in an absolute orgy of repentence.'
'Are you speaking about when she was a child?'
'In a way. But all that happened when she grew up was that the moods didn't come quite so often, but when they did they were that much more intense.'
'And on this island she had such moods?'
'I can't really answer that — I've seen so little of her because she lived at the back of beyond. But you can take it from me that that's how she was before she moved out here . . . Have you any idea why she committed suicide?'
'She left this note in which she said she believed she had cancer. A friend of hers died recently after many months

of pain and the señorita wrote that she could not face such agony.'

'She always was a bit of a hypochondriac.'

'Her friend who died was called Pat. Do you know who this could be?'

'Pat? . . . I've never heard Gertie refer to anyone by that name.'

Alvarez thought for a moment, then drained his glass and stood. 'Señor, you have been most kind and helpful.'

'Just before you go, satisfy my curiosity, will you? Who told you we'd known each other practically all our lives?'

'Until you told me, I was not aware of this.'

'Then what brought you here?'

'In the señorita's will, she leaves everything she possesses to you. That suggested you must know her quite well and would be able to help me.'

'She's left everything to me? . . . Good God!'

He appeared to be genuinely surprised, Alvarez thought.

In his office, Alvarez sat behind the desk and tried to sort out the evidence. If the señorita had not committed suicide, she had been murdered: if she had been murdered, there had to be a motive. In her will, West was named sole heir, but her notes made it clear she'd intended to cut him out of her second will. On the face of things, then, here was a motive. But West's surprise on learning about the contents of the will had appeared genuine and was it reasonable to suppose that a man as obviously wealthy as he would murder for the relatively little that he stood to lose if the will were changed? Had any other possible motive come to light? No. Then surely it was clear the señorita had committed suicide? He'd learned that she'd always been mentally rather un-stable . . . Yet Meade had sworn she was not in the slightest depressed — just the opposite — and there were one or two small discrepancies or queries. Added to which, some months ago they'd had that request from England for information, following the death of West's wife in suspicious circumstances. So, for the second time, West was—possibly—connected with a woman who might not have committed suicide as at first sight seemed likely . . .

He must have fuller details of what had happened in England. Yet any request for those must go through Superior Chief Salas's office. And it was not long since Salas had been assured that this was a clear case of suicide.

He leaned down to open the bottom right-hand drawer of his desk . . .

CHAPTER 13

The bedside digital clock rang the alarm. It was an infuriating sound, being so subdued and polite: discreet, apologetic bleeps. Their old alarm clock had gone off with a rude, raucous clatter which seemed so much more appropriate to an early morning call.

Cullon reached over and turned off the alarm. 'I could sleep for another twelve hours,' he muttered thickly.

'Then why in the hell don't you?' said Tina, visible only to the extent of her curly, dark brown hair.

He yawned. 'Because if I don't turn up on time, the D.I. will have my guts for garters.'

She pulled the sheets and blankets down far enough to reveal a small, round, snub-nosed face, touched with elfin humour. 'I think Mr Rifle wants putting down.'

Then she yawned, propped herself up on one elbow, and looked beyond his right shoulder at the clock. 'Hey! It's only a quarter to seven. You've gone and set the blasted thing half an hour too early. I could get a divorce for that.'

He sat up and ran his fingers through his tangled hair. 'I told you last night, love, I've got to be at the station early.'

'You didn't tell me anything of the sort.'

'When I got back last night . . .'

'You were so exhausted you collapsed in the chair and went to sleep. I woke you up and you managed to eat supper, then you snored your way through the ballet on telly. And when we came to bed, you fell asleep just as I was getting ready to say a very loving good-night.'

He grinned.

'It's not funny,' she shouted.

'Of course not,' he assured her. 'As a matter of fact, I suppose I was a bit tired . . .'

'You weren't a bit tired, you were totally exhausted. Like you've been for weeks. You come home and can't do anything but fall asleep. Our marriage has as much romance left in it as last week's fish and chips.'

'I'm sorry. It's just that we've had a hell of a lot of work . . .'

She was normally a cheerful, happy-go-lucky woman with a tremendous sense of fun, but worry was beginning to make her sharp. 'And you let that blasted man pile most of it on to your shoulders.'

'Someone's got to cope,' he said defensively.

'Why's that someone always have to be you?'

'It isn't. We're all having to do more than usual.'

'I can just imagine how Mac's wearing himself out with work.'

He could not, in all honesty, claim that Detective-Constable MacAllister was pulling his full weight.

'You're so damned conscientious. Why can't you be more like him and regard everything as a bit of a joke?'

'It's just . . .' He stopped.

'I know, it's just you.' She reached over and hugged him. 'And it's just you I love. But I can't bear seeing you wear yourself out. If you go on and on at this rate, you're going to crack up.'

'There's no call to worry. I'm all right.'

'No, you're not, not when you shut your eyes and fall fast asleep as I'm putting on my sexiest nightie. Stop being so blasted conscientious. You can't work miracles all on your own.'

'I know, but . . .'

'Always that but!' She kissed him. 'Suppose I just won't let go of you now for a couple of hours?'

'I'll have a hell of a job explaining to the old man why I'm late.'

'You could tell him the truth.'

'He'd never accept the excuse that a wife could stop a husband doing anything.'

Her sharp anger returned. 'I was talking to his wife at the last social and she told me something that absolutely horrified me. Their last three holidays have been ruined because each time something's turned up at the last moment and he's refused to go away. How can any man be so damned selfish?'

'I suppose he's not very good at delegating the final responsibility in a serious case.'

'He's no good at knowing how to live.'

She studied him as he climbed out of bed and she saw the signs of strain in his face. 'Tim, dead serious for a minute. You've got to learn to take things more quietly.'

'They'll ease up when Cocky comes back from the course and Steve's passed fit for duty again.'

'You're not really understanding a word I'm saying. It's not just the quantity of work you do, it's as much your attitude to it. You've got to learn to worry less.'

'You're right. But if I don't get away from here very soon . . .'

She picked up a book from the bedside table and hurled it at him. It missed.

He chuckled. 'We got called out last week to a woman who had a badly swollen eye and bruised cheeks. But when we wanted to charge the man, she wouldn't give any evidence: said it was only when he beat her up that she could be certain he really loved her. Now I understand what she meant!'

Divisional HQ consisted of a small central building, built sixty years before, to which had been added a number of extensions: since there had never been any overall coherent architectural plan, the complex now resembled a rabbit warren. Everyone agreed a new HQ should be built; no one was prepared to finance this.

Rifle worked in a small, draughty room on the second floor of one of the oldest wings. He looked up from his battered, work-covered desk and saw Cullon yawn. 'Overworked and tired?'

'Yes, sir.'

'That's what I like to hear.' He stared at a point deep in space, to the right of Cullon's head. 'Do you remember Gertrude Dean?'

'Yes, of course.'

'The report's come through that she's just died. Apparently it was a case of suicide.'

Cullon whistled. 'Conscience! It finally caught up with her that she'd saved that bastard by giving him a false alibi.'

'It happened in Mallorca, where she's been living for some time now, as you know. Have you ever been to the island?'

'Never had enough days off together to go anywhere.'

Rifle smiled sardonically. He leaned back in his chair. 'I went there for a week, a few years back. The weather was perfect and there wasn't a cloud in the sky for a whole week. On the first day I got so badly sunburned I had to stay indoors for the rest of the stay. Still, the drink was incredibly cheap . . . The Spanish police report a problem. Did she in fact commit suicide or was she murdered?'

Cullon spoke excitedly. 'West! We heard he'd moved there. For some reason she was going to recant on his alibi and he killed her to keep her mouth shut.'

'Before you let your enthusiasm run too far ahead, all we know for certain is that there's a query over the nature of her death and the Spanish police have asked for some help. They want a full résumé of the facts surrounding the death of West's wife and evidence on what kind of a person Miss Dean was — was she neurotic, given to fits of depression, did she ever threaten to commit suicide . . . Who can help us there?'

'As far as I could ever make out she knew very few people . . . But she did mention once that she had a daily in to do the housework because she loathed dusting and cleaning. The daily might be able to help. Only thing is, I've no idea who she was. Shall I tell Mac to make enquiries?'

'It'll be best if you handle everything.'

Cullon, remembering what Tina had said that morning, cleared his throat. 'I'll have my hands full preparing the résumé . . .'

Rifle jerked himself upright, picked up a single sheet of paper, and read what was typed on it. After a while, Cullon left. There were many aspects of his work which Tina didn't really understand.

Cullon drove out to Queenswood Farm and parked in front of the garage. As he climbed out of the car, he noticed that the drive had recently been resurfaced, the sides of the shed had been tarred and the windows and corrugated tin roof painted, and the five-bar-gate into the front paddock was new. The garden had been altered and now there were geometrically shaped and placed flower-beds and the lawn was immaculate, looking like a bowling green. All the house doors and windows had been painted an interesting shade of puce. He was not surprised to be greeted at the front door by a woman who was dressed as if off to a cocktail party in Hampstead.

She did not ask him into the sitting-room, but kept him standing in the hall. Her voice was drawling, high-pitched, and condescending. 'Yes, I know the woman you mean. As a matter of fact, she worked for me for a while after we moved in, but she really was rather too . . . too familiar, even for this day and age.'

'Can you give me her name? And have you any idea where she lives?'

'Her name's Randall and she lives somewhere in Nearington: I've no idea exactly where. Perhaps in one of the council houses.'

'Thanks a lot for all your help.'

She nodded.

He returned to his car and drove away. Gertrude Dean would surely have been very bitter to learn exactly what kind of people had bought her house, which she had so plainly loved and cherished.

Nearington was a village which had quickly expanded when the main line railway had been electrified to bring it within commuting distance of London: as it had grown it had lost its character and now it was a sprawl of modern houses and bungalows, grouped around the few original homes which looked out of place with their bowed, peg-tile roofs and inaccurate walls.

He stopped outside the general store, now a mini supermarket. The woman behind the till told him that Mrs Randall lived up the road at Cherry Tree Cottage. He drove a couple of hundred yards further on, then turned off to the right and went down the second of three access roads which served the housing estate. Cherry Tree Cottage was the last bungalow on the right and because the land beyond sloped away, there was an attractive view over the surrounding and well wooded countryside.

Mrs Randall was a solidly built woman in her middle fifties who had the determined, though not aggressive, manner of someone who always knew her own mind and was quite ready to express it.

'I don't know whether you've heard that unfortunately Miss Dean has died?' he said.

'Dead?' She stared at him with shocked surprise. 'But she was no age.'

'It seems she may have committed suicide.'

'Poor woman,' she said softly.

'What I'd like to do is have a word with you about her — if you wouldn't mind?'

If she realized that the circumstances of Gertrude's death could not be completely straightforward, she gave no indication of this. 'I liked her and was sorry when she went to live abroad. Worked for her for over two years: ever since my youngest started at the mill and I didn't know what to do with myself all day long. Many's the time she and me have had a joke together.' She paused, then said abruptly: 'How'd you like a cup of tea?'

'Very much indeed.'

'Won't mind having it in the kitchen, will you? But I'm half way through doing the front room.'

The kitchen was spotlessly clean and tidy. She told him to sit at the table in the small eating area while she prepared things. After plugging in the electric kettle, she put a tin of biscuits on the table. 'They're home made, which is why they're all different shapes, but my Bert says they taste all right for all that.'

He ate one and told her it tasted delicious, much to her obvious pleasure.

The tea made and poured out, she sat opposite him.

She began to nibble at a biscuit with the guilty hesitation of someone who was breaking a self-imposed diet.

'I wonder if you can describe what kind of a person Miss Dean was?' he asked.

'Nice,' she replied immediately. 'You know, friendly and never putting on airs because she was paying me for the work.'

That, he thought, was a reference to the new owner of Queenswood Farm. 'Would you say that generally she was a cheerful person?'

'Sometimes she was, sometimes she wasn't. To tell the truth, I used to wonder if she suffered from something like migraine, but she never mentioned it.'

'She was sometimes depressed?'

'That she was. But as she once said to me, if you're an artist you get depressions. She reckoned it was just part of creating.' In a fit of absent-mindedness, she picked out another biscuit from the tin. 'I remember one day when she hardly spoke all morning. I told her, she ought to see a doctor. Only time she was ever rude. Thing is, she didn't have much time for doctors and no one can blame her for that. Treat you like you're just a nuisance, if you give 'em half a chance.'

'So as far as you know, she never sought medical advice over those bouts of depression.'

'Wouldn't think she ever did.'

'Tell me, did she have lots of friends?'

'No, she didn't, and if you want my opinion that's half the reason for her being the way she was. Stands to reason you get to feeling depressed if you never see anyone. Leastwise, that's how I see it.'

'She knew Mr and Mrs West, though?'

'That's right.'

'They were good friends?'

'If you was to ask me, I'd say anyone's a good friend of his when he wants something.'

'One last question, Mrs Randall. Did you ever hear her talk about committing suicide?'

She shook her head. 'Never. And what's more, if you hadn't told me, I wouldn't have believed it possible. I'd've said she was too . . . don't quite know how to put this, but even when she was depressed, she was still fighting.'

'So you wouldn't ever have expected her to commit suicide?'

'That's right. But I mean, how can you tell for sure? There was Mary, what lived in one of the old cottages. Always smiling, helping out: hanged herself one night and from then until now no one understands why. As I always say, there's never any knowing how the other person's going to act . . . How about some more tea? There's plenty in the pot.'

Rifle was still at his desk, working at papers. 'Dug up any pay-dirt?' he asked, without bothering to look up.

'Not really,' replied Cullon. 'I found the daily woman, name of Randall, but she couldn't help except to suggest that even though Miss Dean suffered from depressions, she wasn't the kind of woman to commit suicide.'

'Who can judge?'

'That's just what Mrs Randall said.'

'I'm grateful for the confirmation.' Rifle finally looked up. 'Your wife phoned me earlier on.'

'Is something wrong?' Cullon asked with immediate concern.

'That depends on your definitions. The call was to accuse me of grossly overworking you during the past weeks.'

'Oh!' said Cullon weakly.

'She said I was criminally careless about exploiting you.'

'I . . . I'm afraid, sir, she's been rather upset recently.

You see, I keep telling her I'll be back at such and such a time and then overrun by hours because something crops up.'

Rifle stared through the window at the rain-washed world outside. 'It's hell on the wives and it takes a special kind to survive. Tina will survive. Tell her from me I solemnly promise that the moment work eases up I'll see you get all the leave that's due to you.'

'Perhaps if I could give her a definite date?'

Rifle smiled sardonically. Then he said: 'Have you drawn up the résumé for the Spanish police?'

'I've hardly had time . . .'

'Don't take all week.' He stretched his arms, then stood and began to pace the floor. 'You know, when we couldn't land West for the murder of his wife, I'd have liked to take the laws of evidence and shove them in front of all the judges and ask them if they were happy with a murderer getting away with a fortune because, although the truth was obvious, there just wasn't the legal proof of it that they would demand . . . I'd feel a whole lot happier now if I knew that West was sweating out a life-sentence in a Spanish jail because of a second murder. But we know he's a cunning bastard and from what I saw of the island, everyone on it is three-parts asleep. So there's no reason to imagine the police there will begin to pull their collective fingers out. If West was too smart for us, he'll be ten times too smart for them.'

'There's not much we can do about that.'

'How's your work load?'

'Twice as heavy as I can possibly cope with.'

'I want you to go out to Mallorca.'

'Do what?' said Cullon, voice high with surprise.

'Work with the police. Show 'em the ropes, jolly 'em along, but make certain that if it's humanly possible they land West. Just one word of warning. They're full of that machismo lark so you'll have to let 'em think they've had all the bright ideas, even if you've had to lead 'em by the hand and solve the case from beginning to end.'

CHAPTER 14

The plane landed on the single runway of Aeropuerto de Son San Juan and then followed an open jeep to its parking bay. The passengers disembarked and two buses drove them the short distance to the arrival area of terminal A. They filed through immigration — one bored man who didn't bother to look at the immigration cards he collected — into the arrival hall. Cullon, with only an overnight bag, didn't need to wait for the luggage to come through on the carousel and he walked towards the exit doors where a Customs officer sat on one of the search tables and stared moodily into space.

Cullon walked past the Customs officer and through the doorway, then eased his way past the waiting relatives, friends, and couriers, to come to a stop as he looked around for the uniform policeman he had been assured would meet him.

'Señor Cullon?'

He turned, to face someone older than himself, considerably shorter and plumper, who had the sad, disillusioned face of a man who had long since learned to expect little from life. He was dressed in a crumpled shirt, crumpled linen trousers, and a pair of sandals.

'It is indeed a pleasure to meet you, señor. I am Enrique Alvarez.'

'*Inspector* Alvarez?'

'That is right. We had a conversation on the telephone.'

God Almighty! Cullon thought. When Rifle had called

them sleepy, he hadn't known the half of it.

'Let me take your case?'

'That's quite OK, thanks. It's no weight.'

'If you're sure . . . Shall we go out to the car?'

Cullon pulled his thoughts together. 'There's one thing I ought to do before we leave and that's book my return flight — I thought it better not to do that until I'd had a word with you to find out how long we're likely to be tied up on the case. I want to return to work as soon as possible.'

Alvarez showed his surprise. It seemed an extraordinary thing to want to do.

'Is the evidence complicated?'

'In a way, I suppose it is. And yet it appears it is not.'

So what in the hell did that mean? At all costs, be tactful. 'Perhaps it would be better if I left the booking just for the moment?'

'Indeed.'

Alvarez had borrowed a Seat 124 from the Guardia and this was now parked in the middle of the taxi rank, causing the taxi drivers to swear. He opened the front passenger door. Then he said, almost diffidently: 'Señor, it is hot today. Perhaps for the journey you might feel happier without a coat or a tie?'

When in Rome, wear a toga . . . Cullon took off his tie and coat and put them on the back seat, together with his mackintosh and overnight case.

Alvarez started the engine and, without any signals, drove away from the pavement immediately in front of a tourist bus. 'Have you been on the island before, señor?'

'The name's Tim.'

'Thank you,' he said gravely.

'No, I've never been here before.'

'It is the most beautiful island in the world.'

Cullon noticed a hoarding from which part of the poster was peeling away and flapping in the slight breeze.

'If you could just run through all the facts as you see 'em, I'll go through our end of things and we can compare notes.'

'D'you mean we do that now?'

'That'll save time, won't it?'

Alvarez looked at Cullon, his expression perplexed, then back at the road just in time to avoid hitting the car he was overtaking. 'It will not be very easy when I am driving . . .'

He called this driving? Cullon judged they'd missed that car by less than six inches.

'I wondered which hotel to book you in, Tim. There are some in the port which are very nice, but I decided you would prefer to be at Cala Roig. The scenery is so wonderful. I have spoken to the manager and explained that you must have the best room, facing the sea. It is so relaxing to sit out on the balcony and look at the sea and the mountains.'

Cullon smiled. 'I doubt I'll have much time for sitting around.'

'The swimming there is very good unless there is a strong north wind and then it can be dangerous because of the . . .' He thought for a moment. 'The undertow,' he said proudly. 'But if there is any fear of that, a red flag is flown and a white rope is drawn across the bay to show where it becomes unsafe. Do you like swimming?'

'Yes, very much. But, you know, if I'm to get through the work as quickly as possible . . .'

'I will take you to Parelona beach. Nowhere else in the world is so beautiful. That is, of course, unless one goes on a day when the buses with all the tourists arrive . . . I am sorry to say this, but some of the tourists can be rather noisy.'

The first two-thirds of the drive, along the main Playa Neuva road, were through uninteresting countryside, but then they turned off on to the Llueso road and immediately the land became scenic with tree-covered slopes and later an impressive skyline of stark mountain crests. They rounded the base of Puig Antonia, with its hermitage on top looking like a nipple on a firm breast and as near to heaven as mortal man had been able to reach, to come into sight of Llueso.

'There!' said Alvarez, taking both hands off the wheel to gesticulate. 'There we are!'

Cullon—once Alvarez was once more gripping the wheel—stared at the town (he was to learn that the locals always called it a village), which looked as if the houses had been emptied out over the hill and left to find their own level.

Alvarez checked his watch. 'That's good. We will be just in time.'

'To question West?'

'To eat lunch.'

'There's absolutely no need to bother as far as I'm concerned. A sandwich will do me fine.'

'A sandwich! For your first meal on the island?'

'It's all I ever have when I'm working.'

Alvarez looked at him with evident sympathy, then finally regarded the road once more. 'I hope you do not mind, but I have arranged for us to eat lunch with my cousin. I live with her and her family.'

To object further could only sound rude or boorish, perhaps both. 'That'll be wonderful,' Cullon replied, hoping that MacAllister had been joking when he'd said that snails were one of the favourite dishes on the island.

They turned off the main road and entered the village by way of a maze of narrow streets where, as far as Cullon could judge, traffic wasn't regulated by any rules whatsoever. Bikes and mopeds used whichever side of the road was more convenient, cars jockeyed for position with all the finesse of rampaging bulls, and to reach Calle Juan

Rives they went up a one-way street the wrong way, finally to park in front of a sign which said that in the second half of the month parking was permitted only on the other side of the road.

Cullon climbed out and looked at Alvarez's home. Like every other house in the road, it was terraced with the front door opening directly on to the road and the windows shuttered so that it looked deserted. He remembered the state of terrace houses he'd been inside in England and the gloomy thought occurred to him that even then their luncheons might well be climbing laboriously up the walls inside.

He entered a room twice the size he had expected, spotlessly clean, attractively furnished, and smelling only of polish. He was introduced to the family. Dolores, raven-haired, handsome, received him in so stately a manner that he all but bowed: Jaime smiled and smiled and made a long and involved speech of welcome of which he didn't understand a word: Juan and Isabel, after a brief initial shyness, plied him with questions which Alvarez translated.

'What will you drink?' Alvarez asked him, once he was seated in the nearest, very comfortable, armchair.

'Nothing, thanks. I never have anything when I'm working.'

'But it is the custom to have a drink when one welcomes a friend into the house. Surely you will take something?'

In fact, he realized, he was quite thirsty. 'I'd hate to break a custom! Could I have a very small gin and tonic, please?'

He was handed an embarrassingly large gin and tonic.

They talked—it was not nearly the labour he'd expected, considering everything had to be translated—and after a while he sneaked a look at his watch and was uneasy when he realized how much time had already been wasted, especially in view of the fact that Dolores hadn't

yet even left to start preparing lunch. Alvarez misunder-
stood the cause of his concern and after apologizing for
such a lapse of hospitality, refilled his glass.

Dolores never cooked better than when she thought
she might be severely judged. The gazpacho, made early
that morning, was served with chopped onion, tomato,
cucumber, sweet pepper, and croutons. Jaime offered
white wine and Cullon, who liked wine but seldom could
afford to drink it, said he would like just a little. To his
amazement, the tumbler in front of him was filled almost
to the brim.

The soup was followed by lechona. The spiced
crackling of the sucking-pig was as crisp as newly made
buttersnaps and the meat as tender as a virgin's kiss.
Jaime said he'd have some red wine, of course, and he
could not resist: just a little. His tumbler was filled.
Later, it was refilled.

Strawberry spongecake, buried beneath an avalanche
of whipped cream. The slice he was given would have fed
both Tina and himself. A little white wine to help it
down?

They returned to the front room and sat, except for
Jaime who went over to the long, low, ornately panelled
sideboard, where he opened the right-hand door. He
spoke and Alvarez translated. 'Will you have coñac,
Cointreau, Benedictine, apricot brandy, or chocolate
liqueur?'

'Nothing more: I just couldn't,' he answered, aware
that he was not enunciating his words as clearly as he
would have liked.

'You must have a coñac. Nothing is so good for the
digestion.'

They drank a toast to England and one to Mallorca:
one to the world-famous Scotland Yard (impossible to
explain the difference between the Metropolitan Police
and a county force) and one to the Mallorquin Cuerpo

General de Policía: one to good wives and bad women . . .

Cullon awoke. Something was odd — apart from the taste
in his mouth — and he tried to work out what. Then he
opened his eyes and found he was sprawled out in an
armchair and that on the table to his right was a glass half
full of brandy. My God, he thought, with the horror
which another man might suffer on discovering his wife
was dining at the same restaurant as he and his mistress,
he'd fallen asleep after lunch!

Alvarez entered the room, a welcoming smile on his
broad face.

Cullon struggled to his feet. 'I'm most terribly sorry,' he
said thickly.

'Sorry for what?'

'I'm afraid I fell asleep.'

'But of course.'

'I've never done such a thing before, not in working
hours.'

'Surely you always have a siesta?'

'Never.'

'Then what do you do after each lunch?'

'I work, of course.'

Alvarez shook his head in perplexity. 'Soon, we will go
along to your hotel and make certain all is well. But first,
perhaps, you would like some coffee?'

He would like some coffee very much.

His hotel room was on the top floor, obviating the
common problem in tourist hotels of someone overhead
deciding to dance the Charleston at three in the morning.
The assistant manager, who showed them to the room,
assured Cullon in fluent English that if the slightest thing
was wrong, or if he wanted anything, he had only to
speak.

After the assistant manager had left, Alvarez said:

'Evaristo will make very certain you are completely comfortable. He knows that I know that he's building a house without the proper permissions.'

Cullon, not quite as shocked as he might have been a few hours earlier, wondered what Detective-Inspector Rifle would say concerning the undoubted advantages of misprision.

Alvarez, who had a plastic carrier bag in his right hand, walked out on to the small balcony and stared down at the flat calm sea. 'Shall we change into our costumes?'

'But I'm afraid I haven't brought one with me. I reckoned there'd be no time for swimming.'

'No matter. I'll telephone Evaristo and tell him you need a pair of trunks immediately. He will find you some.'

The sun warmed the whole of Cullon's body as he lay on the towel and with a gesture that went straight back to childhood he scooped up sand with his toes which stretched out beyond the towel. There were the sounds of approaching people and he opened his eyes. Three young ladies, one blonde, two brunette, spread out towels and sat a couple of metres from him. They removed the tops of their bikinis.

A policeman's life was different in Mallorca.

CHAPTER 15

On Monday morning, Cullon awoke at 7.10. Eager to make up for all those wasted hours the previous day, he climbed out of bed, crossed to the window, drew the curtains, opened the shutters, and stepped out on to the balcony. The bay was backed by bleak mountains which rose steeply out of the intensely blue water, making the scene a memorable one. He was tempted to continue to enjoy it, but overcame such weakness and returned inside to wash and dress.

Breakfast was served, at the guest's option, either in the bedroom or by the pool. After a quick shower, he went down to the ground floor and out to the poolside. A yawning waiter reluctantly said he'd check if it were possible to serve breakfast yet and left. A quarter of an hour later, he returned with a tray on which were two ensaimadas, apricot jam, butter, coffee, sugar, and milk.

For once, Cullon ate slowly, enjoying the novelty of breakfasting out of doors, by a pool and the sea. He was surprised to discover, after finishing his second cup of coffee, that the time was already 8.20. He hurried inside to the reception desk and asked if Inspector Alvarez had been looking for him? The gravely courteous receptionist replied that the inspector had not yet arrived. Cullon, as he often did when irritated, jingled the coins in his trouser pocket.

'Sir,' said the receptionist, 'please sit down outside and rest. When the inspector is here, we will tell you.'

He hesitated but, since there seemed to be no reasonable alternative, finally accepted the advice. He crossed the road to the sea patio, built up a couple of metres above sea level, and sat at one of the tables.

Nine o'clock. He stood and stared across the road at the hotel. Had Alvarez forgotten their arrangement for the morning? Surely, even here, that wasn't really possible? Or was it? Perhaps he ought to phone . . . It occurred to him that he didn't know the telephone number, the address, or even Dolores's and Jaime's surname . . . After a while, he settled back in the chair and watched a yacht ghost along with a spinnaker which kept threatening to spill. His eyelids became heavy . . .

'Good morning, Tim. I hope you had a pleasant night?'

Cullon came hurriedly to his feet. 'Haven't slept so soundly in years.'

'Excellent!' beamed Alvarez, as he sat. He waved his arm. 'This is still a most beautiful bay. Yet I can remember it when there were just a few fishermen's huts and if you looked around yourself you could believe the world was still just starting. Now, though . . .' He indicated a number of small, ugly houses, built on a precipitous stretch of rockface on the far side of the bay. 'Now there is building everywhere. Yet they make many people rich. Are the rich happy? Certainly, the poor seldom are . . . I am a fool to talk like this when you are on holiday and trying to enjoy yourself.'

'Hardly on holiday,' corrected Cullon.

Alvarez called a waiter over. 'Two coffees.' He turned to Cullon. 'And you will have a coñac with your coffee?'

'Not this early in the morning, thanks.'

'But it is an old Mallorquin custom which helps a man prepare himself for the day.' Alvarez ordered two Soberanos.

Cullon checked the time yet again. 9.34 and they still hadn't even begun work. He looked at the sea, the mountains, the limitless sky, and suddenly thought: What the hell?

When they were seated in his car, Alvarez said: 'We will question Señor West, of course, but first I thought that perhaps you might like to look in Señorita Dean's house?'

'That would be an idea. Apart from anything else, it'll give me a direct picture of the background.' Cullon sounded enthusiastic. He'd been wondering how on earth to engineer a visit to the house without making it seem that he had absolutely no faith in the other's ability to carry out a proper search.

'And you might find something that I have missed.'

'No way. There's no chance of that.' Alvarez was so

generously guileless that Cullon momentarily felt embarrassed by his own attitude.

They drove the back route to Caraitx, along lanes which wound their zigzag way through undulating countryside. In the village, Alvarez stopped at the municipal police station to collect the key to No. 15, after which they continued up to Calle Padre Vives.

Already the house smelled of disuse and — ironically, since there had been no rain for weeks — of damp. They went upstairs.

'This was the señorita's bedroom. Since her death, nothing has been altered except that I folded up the clothes there, on the chair, and I tidied the bedclothes. The suicide note and the bottle of sleeping tablets are on the table, together with the plastic bag which was taken off her head.'

Cullon went over to the bedside table and looked down at the typed note. After a while he reached out, only to stay his hand. 'I presume the note's been checked for prints?'

'Not yet, no.'

'Why ever . . .' He cut the words short.

'One could not be certain it was necessary,' explained Alvarez.

By leaning over, Cullon could read the note without having to touch it. 'Has anyone heard her recently complaining of pain?'

'Señor Meade and his two friends agree she never once mentioned it. Señora Garcia, who used to work here, says the same. But Señor West refers to her as a hypochondriac.'

'She mentions her friend, Pat, who died. Have you found the letter telling her about the death?'

'No, I haven't.'

'Or any letters from Pat?'

'She has kept many letters, but there is not one from Pat.'

'Interesting, point! . . . Any idea where her typewriter is?'

'In the cupboard over there.' Alvarez pointed. 'The compartment nearest the window.'

'Presumably you've checked that for prints and the type?'

'Not yet.'

'Perhaps . . .' said Cullon, finding it more and more difficult to remain patiently tactful.

Alvarez went over to the cupboard and brought back the Olympia typewriter, which he put on the bed. He opened the case, then threaded a sheet of notepaper into the roller and used the blunt end of a ballpoint pen to tap out the first words of the suicide note. He pulled the notepaper free, looked at it briefly, handed it to Cullon.

Cullon lifted up the suicide note by holding the edges, dropped it on to the bed face uppermost: he spread out the second sheet of paper alongside it. 'Two peas in a pod. First he murdered her, then he sat down and typed out the so-called suicide note. He's a cool bastard, if he's nothing else.'

He turned his attention to the plastic bag. 'Presumably this hasn't been checked out either?'

'I'm afraid it hasn't.'

It was like working with a probationary constable in his first week of duty. 'D'you think it could be arranged for things to be checked?'

'But of course.'

'You don't mind if now I just have a bit of a search?'

'Whatever you wish.'

On the dressing-table Cullon saw the several different sized and shaped pieces of broken earthenware. 'Any idea what this lot was?'

'The pieces were on the floor when I first entered. I'm

certain it was what we call a cazuela—they are dishes which come in many sizes and are used for cooking and other things. When one has tapas in a bar . . . That reminds me. I must take you to the new bar in Llueso. Even though the owner comes from Madrid, his tapas are excellent. I've certainly never tasted better. Kidneys in sherry, meat balls, squid, liver . . .'

'That sounds great. From the look of the inside of these bits, there wasn't anything in the dish when it got smashed. Could've been intended as an ashtray, I suppose. D'you know if she smoked?'

'I am afraid I cannot say.'

'I doubt it's of any importance.' Cullon moved on to the opened window and put his head outside. When he brought his head back in, he said: 'Did the people next door hear anything at all?'

'The mother sleeps at the back of the house and she went to bed early. The son was studying in the front bedroom and says he didn't consciously hear any car stop here. I doubt he would have noticed anyway.'

'So there's no joy there. Did Miss Dean lock all outside doors at night?'

'It is impossible to be certain now, but one must assume that she did. Ten years ago it would not have been necessary: then one did not need to lock anything. But things have become different.' Alvarez sighed.

'So if West had to break in, as opposed to her letting him in, he either needed the key or the skill to force the lock.'

'I don't suppose the lock on the front door is very complicated.'

'Are there any signs of it being forced?'

'I have not had time to check that.'

Cullon was hardly surprised. 'How about doing that before we leave?'

'I think that perhaps I have a lock probe in the car,'

said Alvarez doubtfully.

Cullon left the window and resumed his search. He was very thorough. Alvarez watched him with endless patience.

'That's that, then,' he said finally.

They went through to the studio where Cullon studied the three unframed paintings leaning against one wall. 'These are all right—got lots of colour. Not like the ones she had in her place back home: they were all greys and blacks. But apparently people bought 'em, which just goes to prove not everyone has the same taste.'

'Señor Meade says that since she lived here, she has been happy. Perhaps that is why her paintings now have colour.'

'Could be, I suppose.'

'But then why should the painting on the easel be so . . . so tortured?'

'How d'you mean?' Cullon moved across the floor to study the unfinished painting on the easel. 'It is a bit grim when you get down to it, isn't it? She must have suddenly started feeling blue.'

'Because she believed herself ill, perhaps?'

'Now we're moving outside my horizons! But I do know this much: if she was feeling grim it's ten to one at least part of the trouble was that she'd finally realized West was gunning for her.'

They moved into the spare bedroom, then from there to the bathroom. Downstairs, in the kitchen, Cullon checked the sizes of the plastic bags.

Five minutes later, the search was completed. 'So all that's left to do now,' said Cullon, 'is to check the front door lock to see if it was forced.'

They went out to the car and Alvarez searched through the jumble of things on the back seat, but failed to find the pencil-thin probe. Then, as a last resort, and only after a struggle, he lifted up the bench seat. The probe lay there, together with bits of paper, fluffs of dirt, and several lengths of string. He picked the probe up and switched it on and it failed to light. 'I suppose the battery is finished,' he said philosophically.

'Surely you can get a new one in the town?'

'I suppose so,' he answered wearily.

They drove down the steep roads and finally found an electrical store: this had batteries of every size but the one they needed. Alvarez looked at Cullon, hesitated, then walked along the road to a small corner shop, dark inside and smelling of dried sardines, with open barrels of sugar, rice, flour, and beans. The woman inside took the battery Alvarez handed her, examined it closely, and then asked Alvarez if he came from Llueso. There followed a long discussion, which left Cullon more and more impatient. Finally, however, the woman disappeared through a bead curtain, to reappear a few minutes later with a broad grin of triumph on her face. She handed the old battery back to Alvarez, together with a new one. There was just one remaining problem. She'd no idea how much it cost. Alvarez suggested about fifty-five pesetas and she agreed that that sounded a very fair price.

They returned to Calle Padre Vives and there Alvarez, watched by two interested boys with crude imaginations who commented on what he was doing, inserted the probe into the keyhole of the front door lock and peered down through the lens at the interior mechanism. He slowly revolved the probe, then straightened up and switched off the light. 'I can't see any signs of scratching.' He handed the probe over.

Once he'd focused his gaze, Cullon could see that where the mechanism was not touched by the key the grease and dirt were undisturbed, which made it virtually certain that there'd been no attempt to force the lock. He withdrew the probe, switched off the light, and straightened up. 'If the back door's the same, either he used a key or she let him in.' His voice hardened. 'The second woman to learn too late what kind of a bastard he really is.'

CHAPTER 16

For fifteen years, Quijano had worked in fishing boats, earning so little that there'd been times when he could not afford to buy enough food to feed his family. Then he'd been told that the foreigners, many of whom were now living in the area, were all so stupid that they'd pay ridiculous wages for a gardener. He'd become a gardener.

The woman who'd first employed him had asked if he knew about flowers: he'd assured her that ever since he'd been a youngster he'd been growing hundreds of different flowers and on the whole island no one knew more about them than he. She'd then agreed to pay him what he asked and this had been the final confirmation that foreigners *were* stupid since, naturally, he'd asked for twice as much as he'd expected to get.

He stopped work in the garden of Ca'n Absel and watched a Seat 600 rattle along the dirt track and come to a stop by the garage. Alvarez left it and walked to the front door, rang the bell, and waited. Quijano could have told him that no one was inside, but he continued to watch.

Alvarez turned back and it was then that he first noticed Quijano. He crossed to the steps, climbed down to the pool patio, and came across the lawn to where Quijano stood. 'I'm looking for the English señor.'

'Well, as far as I know he ain't down here,' replied Quijano, with the malicious enjoyment of a cunning peasant playing the part of a fool.

'Is the maid anywhere around?'

'You'd best ask her, not me.'

'I'm from the Cuerpo General de Policía.'

'Think I don't know that?' Quijano hawked and spat.

Alvarez stared more closely at him. 'Miguel Angel!'

'Took you long enough to remember me.'

'All right, but I've not seen you in months and months and I wasn't expecting to find you here.'

They discussed mutual friends, the weather, and the prospect for crops. Eventually Alvarez brought up the subject of West.

'I don't know exactly when he'll be back, but it won't be all that long from now, since he's got to pay me before I go.'

Alvarez leaned against the bole of an orange tree, careful to keep well clear of the lower branches with their deadly spikes. 'What kind of a bloke d'you find him?'

'A foreigner.'

'Yeah. But you can sometimes meet a reasonable one. So is he?'

'I don't let him bother me, if that's what you're getting at.'

'Would you describe him as a nice bloke?'

'If I was too tight to know what I was saying.'

'So what exactly's wrong with him?'

'Acts too big.' He hawked and spat again, to add emphasis to his words.

They heard the sounds of car wheels crunching on a loose surface and looked at the turn in the dirt track: very soon, a Mercedes came into view.

'I'll tell you one thing,' said Quijano. 'He's got a nice car. And come to that, I wouldn't say no to his woman, either.'

'But like as not, she'd say no to you.'

The Mercedes drove into the garage. Alvarez returned across the lawn and up to the house patio.

'You've a great sense of timing!' said West sarcastically.

'OK, so sit down and in a minute I'll get the drinks.'

'I have someone with me, señor.'

'My cellar should just about be able to stretch . . . But you're going to have to wait until I've paid the gardener.'

West walked past Alvarez and down the steps. Alvarez returned to the Seat and spoke to Cullon through the opened window.

They sat on patio chairs, set round the table under the vines. From nearby came the shrilling of cicadas, from further away the toneless clanging of sheep bells. For over a minute, a man in the next field sang, his voice high and wailing, recalling the times of the Moors.

By watching West and Quijano, it was obvious that they were arguing. Then, with an oath that just reached them as a meaningless shout, West brought something from his hip pocket and he handed this over, before turning away and walking back to the pool.

He spoke as he began to climb the steps. 'People are becoming bloody greedier and greedier . . .' His head rose above the level of the patio and for the first time he saw Cullon. He came to a sudden stop.

Cullon, ironically polite, said: 'Good morning.'

'What . . . what are you doing here?'

'Come for a bit of a chat.'

'But . . . but why . . . ?'

'It'll be a lot easier if you can manage to come up to our level.' The play on words was very obvious.

He hesitated, then climbed the remaining steps and by the time he reached the patio he'd managed to regain most of his normal composure. 'I've one golden rule in life. Always put pleasure before business. So what would you both like to drink?'

They both asked for brandy. He went over to the house, unlocked the front door, continued inside.

Quijano, carrying a rubber basket with his mattock in it, climbed up to where they sat. He grinned. 'The stupid bastard couldn't be certain how many hours I worked last week.'

'Worked?' said Alvarez.

Quijano thought that so funny that he was still chuckling when he reached his Mobylette. He secured the basket on to the carrier, making certain the mattock was safe, started the engine, rolled the machine off its stand, sat on the saddle and drove off.

When West returned, he set a silver salver down on the table. He handed round the glasses, sat. He raised his own glass to Cullon. 'Welcome to Mallorca. A country so civilized that even a poor man can afford to drink.'

'And a rich man?'

'I wouldn't know.'

'You should do. Your inherited you wife's estate.'

'But only after the tax man had virtually ruined it.'

'Couldn't you find a way of cheating him?'

'That's hardly fair.'

'Who said I was trying to be?'

'You never understood,' said West, and he sounded more sad than resentful. 'And that makes it all the more tragic. Babs was so scared of losing her dignity through pain that she committed suicide. You've done your damndest to strip the dignity away from her memory.'

'Do you now want us to believe that Miss Dean was trying to maintain her dignity?'

'I don't know what you're getting at.'

'We're interested in the real cause of her death.'

'Isn't that perfectly obvious? She's been mentally unstable ever since she was a kid. She's always been liable to commit suicide.'

Cullon looked at Alvarez, but Alvarez was staring out across the terraced garden and it seemed obvious that he was perfectly content to leave the questioning to the English policeman. 'Maybe she could have . . . But in the end she didn't.'

'Then her death was an accident?'

'No. She was murdered.'

'Murdered! That's impossible!'

'Why?'

'Why? Why in the hell should anyone want to murder Gertie?'

'To prevent her finally admitting that you weren't in her house throughout the evening of your wife's death.'

'Christ! Are you trying to say I murdered her?'

'You catch on fast.'

He slammed his clenched fist down on the glass-topped table. 'I don't know a damn thing about her death.'

'You decided to get rid of her because then you'd be completely safe. And you reckoned it would be easy. After all, you'd murdered your wife and we'd never been able to pin that murder on your shoulders in a court of law.'

'I did not kill Babs.'

'Only trouble was—you didn't realize this, of course—you'd become too cocky.' Cullon's tone was contemptuous. 'It's a common failing. A man commits a crime and because the laws of evidence favour the guilty he gets away with it and that makes him reckon he's too clever ever to be caught. So he goes on and commits carbon copy crimes and never stops to realize that repetition creates pattern and a pattern can identify.'

'What pattern is there? Where's there any similarity?'

'You faked your wife's death as suicide and we were never able to wrap the murder round your neck because Miss Dean gave you an alibi. You faked Miss Dean's murder as suicide and used precisely the same method to kill her and try to cover up the killing . . . Tell me, didn't it ever occur to you to introduce even a little variety? Or were you so certain that no one on this island would ever learn about your wife?'

Beads of sweat, evaporating almost at once, gathered

on West's forehead. 'I swear I don't know anything about Gertie's death.'

'Pile the Bibles ten feet high and it won't make any difference.'

'I tell you, I never touched her.'

'Miss Dean died at around ten—the same time your wife died. Is ten your lucky number? Where were you at ten last Monday night?'

'I . . . I was with a friend.'

'Who?'

'My fiancée.'

'What's she ever done to deserve such a fate? What's her name and address?'

'You're not going to drag her into this.'

'You've just placed her slap in the middle.'

'I . . . I've never told her about what happened in England.'

'She's in for some nasty shocks, then. Her name and address?'

'Go to hell.'

Alvarez turned. 'Señor,' he said quietly, 'it will be much easier if you tell us now. Then the matter can be dealt with discreetly.'

West still hesitated, then he said bitterly: 'Rosalie Rassaud.'

'Where's she live?' asked Cullon.

'In the urbanización behind this place.'

'What's the name of the house?'

'Ca'n Piro.'

'How long were you there Monday evening?'

'I was there . . . all night.'

Abruptly Cullon changed the subject. 'How many years had you known Miss Dean?'

For a moment, West seemed bewildered, then he said: 'Ever since we were kids.'

'Where did she live when you first met her?'

'Wealdsham.'

'Can you say what her address was then?'

'The house was in Brick Lane. Number ten . . . twelve . . . I can't remember exactly. What's it matter where she lived?'

The question went unanswered and it was several seconds before Cullon said: 'Why did Miss Dean let you have a key to her house?'

'Who says she did?'

'You're denying it?'

'Of course I'm bloody well denying it,' he shouted. 'I've hardly seen her since I came to live on the island and haven't been within miles of her place, ever.'

'Why did she move out to Mallorca?'

'I wouldn't know.'

'Was it to try and get away from you?'

'Why the hell should she want to do that?'

'Think about it.'

'You're trying . . .' began West hotly, then abruptly stopped speaking.

Alvarez looked at Cullon, who nodded. Alvarez stood. 'Before we depart, señor, will you please give me your passport? You will kindly not try to leave Mallorca until our investigations are completed and you have permission to do so.'

'You've no right . . .' West again became silent. As a foreigner, suspected of murder, it was he who had few rights. He swore, stood, and went into the house. When he returned, he had his passport in his right hand: he dropped it on to the table in front of Alvarez with a gesture of insolent resentment.

Later, as they drove along the dirt track, the suspension of the car thumping heavily, Cullon said, with open satisfaction: 'This time, we've got the bastard running scared.'

CHAPTER 17

Cullon, perspiring so freely that his shirt was sodden and sticking to his back, sat on the edge of Alvarez's desk and dialled 07. He waited for the high-pitched note to indicate he was through to International, dialled 44, and then the eight figures for Petercross divisional HQ. There was a brief rash of high-pitched squeaks — without which no international call ever seemed complete — and then he was through. He asked to speak to the detective-inspector.

'Yes?' said Rifle, sounding as impatient as ever.

'Cullon here, sir.'

'Where's here?'

'Llueso.'

'Why the devil are you still there?'

'Things have turned out to be a little bit complicated.'

'Uncomplicate them.'

'It's not all that easy.'

'What's the matter? Having trouble with the natives?'

Cullon remembered the siesta, the beach, the swim, and the proud, shapely young women. 'Could you organize some information? Find someone who knew Gertrude Dean when she was a youngster and get this person to talk about those times. She used to live in Brick Lane, Wealdsham: possibly number ten or twelve. West maintain's she's always been mentally unstable and I'm hoping you'll be able to shoot down that sort of evidence.'

'It sounds as if you're fairly confident this time?'

'As confident as I can be at this stage.'

'So you've broken whatever alibi he tried to set up?'

'As a matter of fact, no, not yet.'

'Why not?'

'We haven't had time.'

'Not had time? What in the hell have you been doing all the while?'

'Laying the groundwork.'

'You're not out there to build roads . . . . What's the weather like with you?'

'Very sunny and hot.'

'No doubt you'll be pleased to know that here it's raining like the second Flood's starting.'

After the call was finished, Alvarez looked at his watch. 'If we go back now, we'll just have time for a drink before lunch.'

Cullon made no objection.

Rosalie Rassaud was not beautiful, but she was very attractive because honesty, gentle good humour, warm emotions, and a sense of deep loyalty were always attractive. She seldom dieted, yet maintained an enviable figure. She had honey-coloured hair which curled naturally, a high forehead, deep blue eyes, a wide mouth, and a chin just square enough to hint at the fact that she could be very determined, even pig-headed at times. Stupidity, cruelty, or injustice, aroused her anger and when angry she didn't care what she said: a Mallorquin whom she'd found beating his dog with a thick stick had later, and admiringly, referred to her as sounding like a fishwife.

Her husband had been killed a year before in a road accident. She'd been so shocked and so grief-stricken that had she been less strong-minded, she might have contemplated suicide. He had been earning a very good salary, but they'd both been young and careless about the future and when he'd died he'd left her two properties, one in France which was on a heavy mortgage, the other a holiday home in Mallorca bought largely on a bank loan, a few investments, many debts, and beyond that only happy memories. Once her financial affairs had been put into order, she'd been left with only the home in Mallorca and just over a hundred and fifty thousand francs in cash. Obviously, she was going to have to find a job. The thought of working again hadn't worried her, but the thought of being on her own in France had terrified her because she hadn't yet been ready to face the world. So she'd decided to use part of her capital to live for one year in Llueso, after which she'd sell the house and return to France and a solitary working life.

Four months before the date of her return to France, she'd met West. She was too generous in character to wonder what sort of person lay behind that facile charm; nevertheless it was doubtful if normally she would have become very friendly with him. But for her, circumstances weren't normal. And he made her laugh, and even though she was the least mercenary of women, she could not forget that his wealth offered the security she had once had and had then, frighteningly, lost . . .

The urbanización in which she lived stretched from the gently sloping ground at the foot of a mountain to a quarter of the way up its ever-steepening side. The houses high up cost roughly twice as much to build as those below and suffered shifting foundations and cracked walls, but had magnificient views: houses at the bottom normally only suffered minor structural troubles, but they had no views at all since the developer had employed a landscape expert who had preserved all the pines originally on the site and had then planted vast numbers of cypress, oleanders, and cacti, so that all was shade and intrusive gloom. Ca'n Piro, at the bottom, was a bungalow built in Ibicencan style: which was to say, it had graceful curving lines and flat roofs which leaked in heavy rains.

Alvarez led the way to the front door, at the head of a short flight of stone steps, and when Rosalie opened the door he introduced himself and Cullon. 'I am very sorry to trouble you, señora, but we need to ask you some questions.'

They entered. The sitting-room was not large and as this had been a holiday home the furniture was very simple and there was not much of it, but she had used colour with such imagination that no one ever thought of the room as under-furnished. On the mantelpiece above the open fireplace were two framed photographs: one was of her late husband, the other of West.

'Señor West will have told you we would be coming, and why,' remarked Alvarez, more as a statement than a question.

She hesitated. 'He phoned me,' she finally admitted. She spoke English with a slight accent which did not distort her words, but added to them a chuckling charm. She sat very upright in her chair with a loose cover in yellow and red zebra stripes. 'It is ridiculous to believe that Keir knows anything at all about the death of Gertrude.'

'I sincerely hope so; nevertheless I must make certain. The señorita died a week ago, at about ten o'clock on Monday night. Will you tell us, please, if you saw Señor West that evening?'

'Yes, I did. He was here.'

'When did he arrive and how long did he stay?'

'He came at about seven and spent the night.'

'He was here all night?'

'Yes.'

'Thank you, señora.'

Cullon, impatient because he considered Alvarez's questioning to have been far too soft, said: 'Has he ever told you what happened in England before he came to live on the island?'

'He said that his wife had tragically died.'

'He actually used the word "tragically"?'

'Why are you so surprised? Isn't death always tragic?' she asked bitterly.

'That all depends . . .'

'It is always tragic,' interrupted Alvarez. He stood. 'Señora, thank you for all your kindness. I am very sorry if we have distressed you.'

'Surely . . .' began Cullon hotly.

Alvarez again interrupted him. 'Goodbye, señora.'

They left. The moment they were seated in the car, Cullon said heavily: 'I don't know if you realized it, but she was lying as hard as she could go. All we needed to do was tell her West's wife didn't just "tragically" die, she was murdered, and we could have broken her and got to the truth.'

'Perhaps.' Alvarez turned the key and the engine started at the third attempt.

'Then why head me off as you did and just leave?'

Alvarez backed down to the road and turned right, in the direction of the entrance to the urbanización. 'She has known much sorrow.'

'What's that got to do with it?'

'Do you really wish to add still more sorrow until you can be certain it is necessary? What is the truth about the death of Señorita Dean? Suppose we are wrong when we believe West murdered her? Suppose he was not with Señora Rassaud at all that night, yet nevertheless knows nothing about the death of the señorita?'

'Suppose we believe in fairies?'

'Sometimes, I do.'

Exasperated, Cullon looked sideways and to his complete surprise realized from Alvarez's expression that the comment had not been made facetiously. He slumped back in the seat. How could anyone cope on an island where a detective let a vital witness off the hook because he believed in fairies?

They passed a field of orange trees in which a man was

working the soil beneath the trees with a wooden cultivator pulled by a mule: coming along the road in the opposite direction was a donkey cart, driven by an old woman in widow's weeds: just visible, beyond the field to their left, were two women and a man who were winnowing some sort of grain with large wooden shovels. They were, Cullon thought, centuries away from the world of packaged holidays. Perhaps in such a past there were fairies . . . He silently swore. He was in danger of becoming every bit as crazy as the locals.

Alvarez slowly drove up the street in Llueso, stopped suddenly and without warning. There was a brief squeal of brakes. Cullon looked through the rear window and the driver of the car behind tapped his head. 'I think she lives in that house there,' said Alvarez.

Who? wondered Cullon. The ugly witch?

Alvarez saw a vacant parking space and still without any signs made for it and parked. 'I will go and make certain that Francisca does live there.'

Cullon watched him walk past two women, who were sweeping clean the road outside their homes and taking the opportunity to gossip, and enter the house he had previously indicated.

Alvarez returned a moment later. 'She lives here and she is inside, so we can talk to her.'

They sat in the front room, spotlessly clean and smelling faintly of spices. She asked them what they'd like to drink and poured out a couple of brandies. She was about to sit down when there was a call and a young child, just at the walking stage, staggered into the room. She picked him up an settled him on her lap and he stared with wide-eyed curiosity at the two visitors. Cullon was hardly surprised when the first ten minutes of the conversation, conducted in Mallorquin, clearly concerned the child and not the case.

Finally translating all that was said, Alvarez began to question her. 'Was Señorita Dean ever at the señor's house?'

'She's been there, yes.'

'What about recently?'

Francisca tickled the palm of her son's hand to keep him contented. 'I suppose she called a couple of times: something like that.'

'When was this, as near as you can say?'

'The first time was . . . must have been around the beginning of the month and the second wasn't all that long ago. Matter of fact, the señor was out. I told her he almost certainly wouldn't be back for hours, but she insisted on waiting for quite a while.'

'Can you remember anything about the first visit?'

'Only that they had a terrible row. She was shouting so, I thought something awful would happen.'

'D'you have any idea what the row was about?'

'Not really, because they were shouting in English and I don't understand English all that well.'

'Wasn't there a single word you caught?'

She drew out from the short sleeve of her cotton frock a small, lace-edged handkerchief and wiped her son's nose, much to his vocal annoyance. Then she hushed him up before she answered. 'There was some sort of name she kept shouting.'

'What kind of name?'

She thought. 'It wasn't Mallorquin.'

'Could it have been Rosalie?'

She was surprised. 'That's what it was! But how did you know that?'

'It just seemed likely. Did you see the señorita when she left?'

'Yes, but only for a second.'

'How d'you say she looked?'

'Like . . . Well, like someone who's just had terrible

news. Her face was all twisted and she'd been crying. I felt
ever so sorry for her. The señor . . . Well, there are times
when he's not the kindest of men. I know that from
working for him.'

'Thanks a lot for all your help, Francisca.' Alvarez
stood, put his hand in his pocket, and brought out some
loose change, from which he picked out a fifty-peseta
piece. He offered the coin to the boy, who stared at it for
a while before snatching it.

They left and returned to the car. Once settled,
Alvarez began to tap on the wheel with his fingers.

Cullon was determined that there should be no more
talk of fairies. 'It's pretty obvious what happened the
night of the row. Gertrude Dean had learned about the
engagement and went along to West's place to do her
damndest to break it up. She'd have been jealous of Mrs
Rassaud, of course, but far more to the point, bitterly
furious that her over-close friendship with Mrs Rassaud
must suffer if the marriage went ahead.

'West was fool enough to laugh in her face. She
threatened that if he didn't do as she demanded, she'd tell
us back in the UK that he wasn't in her house at the time
his wife died. That left him totally exposed and with only
one way of escape — murdering her . . . Don't you agree
it's time to go back and see Mrs Rassaud again?'

'We must just wait for the evidence from the forensic
laboratory,' replied Alvarez, sadly prevaricating.

CHAPTER 18

The Institute of Forensic Anatomy telephoned at midday
on Tuesday. The post morten on Señorita Dean had been
completed. She had died from asphyxia, entirely
consistent with having a plastic bag over her head. There

were no signs of any bruising, or other injuries, and there were no scrapings under the nails to suggest she had inflicted any defence wounds. She had taken ten grains of seconal shortly before her death. She had not been suffering from cancer.

'The complete carbon copy of Mrs West's murder,' said Cullon, as he stood by the open window in Alvarez's office, trying to cool down. 'So now can we go and tear up that alibi?'

Alvarez scratched the side of his face. 'We still have not heard from the forensic laboratory about the typewriter and the suicide note.'

'You're just goddamn stalling!' Cullon spoke with a measure of frustration, but even so there was a note of understanding sympathy in his voice. He'd only known Alvarez since Sunday, yet in that short time he'd come to like him a lot, despite his obvious incompetence. 'You know, Enrique, you're too sentimental for this job.'

'Perhaps you are right. But I find I can never be certain about some meanings. The meaning of guilt, of murder . . .'

'For Pete's sake, sometimes one can have a bit of an argument about that sort of thing, but not this time. Gertrude Dean was killed to keep her mouth shut — even in a bleeding-heart liberal's book that has to be straight brutal murder.'

'I am getting old and old men often talk nonsenses.'

Cullon grinned. 'It's not just the old. You ought to hear some of the blokes I have to work with back home!' He stepped away from the window. 'Forgetting Mrs Rassaud just for the moment, I've a confession to make. There's one thing that's really been puzzling me about your job, Enrique. Don't you suffer the ordinary run of crimes in this neck of the woods: assaults, drunkenness, thefts, break-ins, that sort of thing? If this were back home, I'd be doing a balancing act with at least a dozen cases over and above the murder.'

'There used to be very little, but recently . . .' Alvarez sighed as he looked at the pile of muddled papers on his desk. 'Recently, there have been so many crimes because people are less honest. Ten years ago there might have been a break-in and theft from a house in a month, now there can be ten in a day. If I tried to deal with everything, I would kill myself with worry and work. So I just concentrate on one case at a time.'

'I wonder how that system would go down back home,' said Cullon.

A member of the forensic laboratory telephoned Alvarez at 7.30 that evening. 'The plastic bag displays one peculiar characteristic and that is a fault across a bottom corner: it's only half a centimetre long, but it is obvious in a good oblique light. There were several fingerprints on the bag, all of which belonged to the deceased. In addition, there are two or three marks which might have been made by gloved hands — can't be any more definite than that.

'We've checked the typewriter for prints and the only one's we've been able to raise are of the deceased. This was not the machine used to type the suicide note.'

'Not?' said Alvarez, his voice sharp with astonishment.

'I know the impressions appear to be similar, but under close examination it's clear they're not. The typewriter you sent us is a new one and none of the letters have begun to show any signs of wear, whereas the suicide note was written by a machine which has seen considerable use.'

Alvarez thanked the caller and said goodbye.

'So he didn't sit down after murdering her and calmly type out the note,' said Cullon slowly. 'He's not as cool as we've been giving him credit for. And when you stop to think about it, something else is also pretty obvious, isn't it? He knew the typing had to appear to have been done on her machine so that any cursory glance would assume it had been—remember, the whole murder was based on the near certainty that there'd be no detailed investigation of an apparent suicide. But he also knew that he had to get hold of a machine exactly similar to hers to do the typing because he could judge that the moment he'd murdered her he was going to have to get out of the house as he wouldn't have the nerve to stick around, not even for the few minutes necessary to do the typing . . . We're going to crack him far more easily than we thought.'

Alvarez said in puzzled tones: 'Perhaps you are right. But he would not confess to the murder of his wife.'

'We never found a way to start really hurting him simply and solely because Gertrude Dean gave him an alibi and all the time he knew that, failing our uncovering direct evidence of his murder, he was laughing . . . Well, do we now go and see Mrs Rassaud and make her tell us the truth, or can you think up yet another excuse for holding back?' He grinned, taking some of the sting out of the words.

They arrived at Ca'n Piro to find Rosalie was out. As they stood by the front door, at the head of the steps, Cullon swore. 'You don't think she's made a bolt with West?'

Alvarez shook his head. 'She would never do that.'

'How can you be certain. She lied like a trooper over the alibi.'

'Because she believes he had nothing to do with the señorita's death. Therefore it cannot be wrong to help him. But to run away with him would be to admit his guilt. She could never ever live with a man who she knew had murdered.'

'All this because of the look in her eyes!' said Cullon, in exasperation.

Fifty metres to their right was another bungalow, only vaguely visible through the growth. Sufficient noise was coming from that direction to suggest some sort of party was in progress.

Cullon said: 'It's a bit of a long shot, I know, but the people living there might just have noticed whether or not West's car was parked here that evening. If we could prove to her we know she's lying . . . Don't you reckon it's worth the effort of finding out?'

They walked down to the road and along to an elaborate entrance with wrought-iron gates. Just inside, built up at its southern end, was a small swimming pool and grouped around this were two men and two women, all in costumes: one couple were lying on towels, the other were sitting on patio chairs. A mobile cocktail cabinet was near the chairs and the pitch and volume of the voices—they were speaking French—suggested that full use had been made of it. As the two detectives walked up the drive and then climbed on to the pool patio the man in the chair, middle-aged, balding but with a mat of hair on his chest, stood.

Speaking in French, Alvarez explained the reason for their call.

'Of course we'll help if we can. But before that, what'll you drink?'

'A coñac would be very nice, señor.'

'And what about your friend?'

Alvarez spoke to Cullon in English. 'He's asking what you would like to drink?'

The man, in an English almost as fluent as Alvarez's, said: 'I have gin, whisky, Bacardi rum, brandy, and sweet and dry vermouth.'

'I'll have a brandy, if I may,' replied Cullon. Everyone a bloody linguist, he thought, suddenly feeling rather inadequate. It was not a feeling to which he was accustomed.

'Let me introduce everyone,' said the man. 'I am Henri de la Sap. Not, I am told, a very flattering name in English!' He laughed very heartily. 'The lady in this chair is my wife. Lying on the towels are Monsieur and Madame Messmer, who have the great misfortune to live in Paris, which is why Monsieur Messmer looks so very ancient.'

They all laughed. They were at the alcoholic stage where even a weak joke was uproariously amusing.

De la Sap poured out two large brandies and added ice. 'No one has found you a chair! Jacques, if you can still stand, fetch these gentlemen two chairs.'

Messmer, at times concentrating very hard on what he was doing, carried over two more patio chairs which he set within the shade of a brightly coloured beach umbrella. Alvarez and Cullon sat: glasses were handed to them.

De la Sap leaned forward. 'Now, satisfy our curiosities. What terrible crime brings you to us? Has someone stolen all the brandy in town?'

Alvarez answered him. 'Señor, can you remember Monday evening, the nineteenth of the month?'

'Can I? Can I not!'

'Almost certainly not,' said his wife.

'I remember everything,' he contradicted loudly. He turned to Alvarez. 'You will understand it was Adèle's birthday and we had a little quiet celebration here.'

His wife said jeeringly: 'He calls it a quiet celebration!'

'It merely shows how little he remembers of what happened,' said Messmer.

Alvarez pointed in the direction of Ca'n Piro. 'Have you met the French lady who lives there?'

'Indeed. A very charming and beautiful young lady. And if Adèle were not on holiday with me . . .'

'She's engaged to be married to a man half your age and twice as handsome,' said his wife scornfully.

'Mature Bordeaux is always more interesting than fresh Beaujolais.'

'Not when it's become corked.'

'How did you come to meet Señora Rassaud?' asked Alvarez.

'On the first day of our holiday,' answered de la Sap, 'the cooker in this place wouldn't work properly and we couldn't get hold of the courier to see if she knew what to do, so I went next door to discover if anyone there could help. The most charming Rosalie came and showed us what was wrong.'

'Did you see her on the night of your wife's party?'

'Indeed. Do you imagine we'd let so charming a compatriot be on her own on such a night?'

'She was in this house?'

Madame Messmer, slightly more sober than the others, suddenly remembered that they were policemen and became worried. 'We've asked her here several times. There's surely nothing wrong in that, is there?'

Cullon spoke with aggressive excitement. 'Can you say what time she came here?'

'I can't be certain, no.'

'Then as near as you can get.'

'Well . . . I suppose it was around seven.'

'And how long was she here?'

'She wouldn't stay to a meal, even though we tried very hard to persuade her. She must have left at . . . about half-past nine?' She looked to the others for confirmation. They said nothing.

'Was anyone with her?'

'No, no one.'

'Did you see her fiancé at all?'

'We asked her to bring him along, but she said he was going to be out all evening . . . Why are you asking all these questions?'

Alvarez answered. 'There is a something which we have

to know, señora, and you have helped us.'

The four were uneasily aware that a matter of importance had been decided, but they had not the slightest idea what.

CHAPTER 19

Rosalie sat in her brightly coloured sitting-room, hands clasped together in her lap. The harsh morning sunlight came through one of the windows on to a part of the tiled floor that was uncarpeted and it was reflected up to touch her hair with sparkling highlights: it also outlined her face too sharply so that her apprehension was obvious. 'I've told you everything I can.'

Alvarez said: 'Señora, yesterday evening we spoke to the four French people who are staying at the next bungalow.'

For a moment she couldn't follow the significance of this, but then she remembered what she had told the detectives on their previous visit.

Alvarez's tone was deeply sympathetic. 'One always wishes to be loyal to people one loves, but unfortunately sometimes that can be wrong. Señora, did Señor West ever discuss with you what happened in England before he came to live on this island?'

'I've told you already. He said his wife died very suddenly and that because of the way the police behaved, her death was made doubly tragic for him.'

'Did he explain further?'

'No. He was far too distressed about it all to say anything more.'

Cullon, who was unable to keep silent any longer, said: 'He was distressed, all right, but not for the reason you think.'

She tried to retain her composure, but now her apprehension had become fear.

'When Mrs West's death was first reported it was treated as suicide. But very soon, we discovered she'd been murdered. The only serious suspect was West, but Gertrude Dean swore that he'd been in her house at the time of his wife's death. We were never able to persuade her to tell us the truth. If we'd succeeded, we'd have arrested him and charged him with the murder of his wife.'

She moved her hands as if trying to push away the terrible facts that were crowding around her.

'Gertrude Dean came and lived on this island and later on—after we'd asked the Spanish police to question her on a point on which we're certain she again lied—West moved out here. Presumably, to make certain she never recanted. Murder is an extraditable offence in Spain and had we gained the evidence we were after, we'd have brought West back to England to stand trial.

'Of course, it was pretty obvious that should Miss Dean die, we almost certainly never would be able to find sufficient evidence . . . She died. And in exactly the same circumstances as West's wife. And once again, we've discovered it wasn't suicide, as at first appeared, it was murder.'

'You're . . . you're lying,' she whispered.

'I wish we were,' said Alvarez sadly.

'Oh God!'

'Señora, perhaps now you can understand why I said earlier that sometimes loyalty to someone one loves can be wrong . . . Please tell us the truth. Did you see Señor West that Monday night?'

She shut her eyes.

'Señora, you must tell us.'

She spoke with violence. 'I didn't see him.' She opened her eyes and stared with hatred at Alvarez. 'He wouldn't

come because he had to go out. I didn't see him at all.'
She began to sob.

Alvarez stood, said with deep compassion: 'Señora, you
need a friend to be with you. Tell me who we can ask to
come here?'

'Get out.'

'Señora . . .'

'Get out. Get out.'

They left.

They were silent from the moment they drove away
until they were passing the football field, then Cullon said
bitterly: 'I'll make the bastard confess, even if I have to
beat it out of him, inch by bloody inch.'

'Only one man. Yet because he is evil, many people are
so badly hurt.'

'But for our goddamn stupid laws of evidence, we'd
have nailed him for killing his wife. Then she wouldn't be
back there, in that bungalow, breaking her heart.'

'That is why I do not always understand what justice
means.'

They turned off the major road in the direction of the
mountains, so that now they were travelling parallel to
the road from the urbanización. They passed irrigated
fields, in each of which grew five or six different crops, an
estanque that was being emptied to feed irrigation water
channels, and four women picking French beans, who
bent double at their work. They reached the dirt track
which took them up to Ca'n Absel.

West was sunbathing by the pool and they judged from
his initial casual reaction to seeing them approach that
Rosalie had not telephoned him about their visit. When
they climbed out of the car, West stood and said: 'You've
at last got your timing wrong. This bar doesn't open
before a quarter to twelve at the earliest.'

'Señor, will you please come up here so we may talk.'

'Why don't you come down here?'

No one moved. West laughed scornfully, bent down, picked up a towel and looped this round the back of his neck. He left the poolside and climbed the steps. 'If Mohammed wasn't too proud to move, why should I be? Well, what's brought you here this time?'

'A few more questions.'

'You've more questions than my tax inspector back home, may he suffer a nasty fate.' He indicated the chairs set around the glass-topped table under the vines. 'If we've got to waste time, why not waste time in comfort?'

They sat.

'Well, what are the questions?'

'Will you tell us, please, where you were on the evening of Monday, the nineteenth?'

West spoke with weary contempt. 'Don't you blokes ever listen? I've told you, God knows how many times, I spent the night with my fiancée. Maybe not according to Emily Post, but times have changed since she was about.'

'We have just come from speaking with Señora Rassaud.'

Like a wild animal first scenting danger, but as yet unable to determine its extent or the direction from which it threatened, West's sardonic manner changed to being sharply watchful.

'We asked her to corroborate your alibi.'

'So now you're finally satisfied that I was with her.'

'On the contrary,' snapped Cullon, his manner in sharp contrast to Alvarez's. 'Now we're satisfied you weren't.'

'Are you trying to call her a liar?'

'Not now. She finally admitted that she didn't see you at all that evening.'

'Like hell she did. If you think you can come here and trick me . . .'

'Save your breath. We also spoke to the French people who've rented the next-door place. She was with them for part of the evening and she was on her own . . .

Understand? No alibi. Not this time.'

'They've got their days mixed up.'

Cullon smiled.

West stared out at the distant bay, careful to keep his face as far as possible turned away from them. 'All right,' he finally admitted, 'I wasn't at her place when I said I was.'

'So where were you?'

Twice he started to speak, twice he checked the words. Then he said curtly: 'Here.'

'Are you now trying to make out you were here all evening?'

'I swear I was.'

'Are you sure?'

'Of course I'm bloody sure.'

'Then how come you told Mrs Rassaud you couldn't be with her because you had to go out?'

'Never mind what I told her. I was here, in the house, all evening.'

'No. You were driving to Caraitx to murder Gertrude Dean because she threatened to recant on your alibi and that would have exposed you as the murderer you are. You had to silence her before she carried out her threat. And because you're not as smart as you imagine, you murdered her in precisely the same way as you murdered your wife.'

'Christ, why won't you ever understand? I didn't kill Babs. I loved her.'

'You loved her money very much more and you were in danger of losing all that because she was changing her will.'

Alvarez said: 'Why did you tell the señora that you would be out all evening and then not go out at all?'

'I . . . I changed my mind.'

'Then why didn't you join her at the party the French people were giving?'

'By then it was too late.'

'Too late to be any use as an alibi?' asked Cullon.

'How could I know I'd ever need an alibi? I didn't go because it was late and I was tired.'

'It wasn't a case of how late it was, was it? What really happened is that you'd just killed Gertrude Dean and discovered your nerves weren't half as strong as you'd thought them.'

'I never went near Gertie's place.'

'Prove it.'

'How can I? I was here, on my own. I didn't see anyone else. But I was here all evening.'

Alvarez spoke. 'Señor, I would like to have your permission to search this house?'

West shook his head, realized from their expressions the futility of this denial, shrugged his shoulders. 'You'll not find a bloody thing,' he said aggressively.

They started in the far, or guest, wing of the house. In the third bathroom, Francisca was washing down the tiled walls. Her curiosity was obvious, but it largely went unsatisfied.

They moved into the central living quarters. Watched by West, who had regained sufficient confidence to jeer at them for wasting time and effort on one of the hottest days of the summer, they quickly but expertly searched for any trace that might prove to be a link between this house and No. 15, Calle Padre Vives.

There were three more bedrooms and bathrooms in the owner's wing, the master bedroom being considerably larger than any of the other five. One wall of this was taken up with a built-in cupboard, which was filled with clothes.

'Quite the Beau Brummell,' said Cullon, fingering a lightweight grey check suit.

'So who's your fat friend?' sneered West.

'Meaning precisely who?' demanded Cullon, his voice suddenly violent.

'No one,' muttered West.

The next bedroom was being used as a study and beyond a partners' desk was a small square table on castors on which stood a portable typewriter. Cullon went straight over to this and opened the lid. 'Now there's an interesting coincidence!' He did not try to hide his satisfaction.

'What is?' asked West.

'This is an Olympia.'

'What of it?'

'Has it been well used?'

'How the hell would I know? I bought it from a bloke who was returning to the UK. What's it matter if it's typed out the London telephone directory?'

'Gertrude Dean had a typewriter and typed out her suicide note. There didn't seem any significance in that until the experts checked and discovered the note hadn't been typed on her machine. I wonder, I do just wonder, if we'll find that the note was typed on this machine?'

'Of course it goddamn well wasn't.'

'Then you won't mind finding me a sheet of typing paper?'

West went over to the desk and pulled open one of the drawers. He brought out several sheets of paper. 'Here. Start a second bloody *War and Peace*.'

Cullon inserted a sheet of paper and wound it down, typed briefly and with some fluency despite only using two fingers, pulled the paper free and studied the typing. He passed the paper across to Alvarez. 'Ten to one in fivers the experts will match it.'

'D'you think if I'd killed her I could be such a fool as to use my own typewriter?' West demanded wildly.

'Yeah. And why? Because, as always happens, you

became too cocky. You'd got away with murder, so in your eyes that made you twice as smart as the police. You could even afford to cut a few corners the second time. And you particularly wanted to cut one of the corners because you knew you wouldn't fancy hanging around Miss Dean's house after you'd murdered her: didn't want her dead eyes watching you.'

'You're bloody crazy.'

They looked through all the papers in the desk and the contents of half a dozen files, but found nothing of interest.

Ten minutes later, when they were back in the air-conditioned sitting-room, Cullon said: 'One final thing — we'll give your cars the once over.' Then, belatedly, he remembered that he was not in charge of the investigations and his manner could easily have given considerable offence. But Alvarez's expression was not one of annoyance, but of perplexity. Privately, Cullon was not surprised. It must be a hell of a struggle for the poor old boy to keep up with events.

They searched the Seat 127 and afterwards the Mercedes. In the bottom of the glove compartment of the Mercedes, beneath the instruction manual, Cullon found a single, scrumpled-up plastic bag.

He smoothed out the bag and held it so that the sunlight caught it at an angle, then passed it across to Alvarez. 'It's the same size as the one over Miss Dean's head. And what was so interesting about that was, wasn't it, that there weren't any other bags of the same size in her house although there were others which she could, and surely would, have used had she really committed suicide.'

'There are millions of plastic bags . . .' began West.

'Not like this one. This has a fault running across one bottom corner. And so did the one used to murder Gertrude Dean. In other words, they came from the same manufacturer's batch. No one's getting to call that just a coincidence.'

West was very frightened.

CHAPTER 20

They drove back along the dirt track, bouncing from pot-hole to pot-hole, and finally reached the metalled road. Cullon said: 'It's a dead cert the lab will match the typed suicide note to his typewriter: and match the two plastic bags. We've finally wrapped up the case.'

'I suppose so,' agreed Alvarez doubtfully.

'What more are you asking for? A signed confession?'

'He was very disturbed by what we found.'

'Is that surprising? He gets away with one murder which turns him into a millionaire and everything in the garden's lovely. But then suddenly he's in danger of being exposed and has to kill again. By now, he reckons nothing's easier. Only it isn't quite so simple.'

'Why was he in such danger that he had to murder a second time?'

Cullon briefly turned to look with tolerant amusement at Alvarez. 'Because Gertrude Dean had threatened to recant on his alibi, of course.'

'But why should she have done that, after standing by him all the time they were in England and even when she first came to live out here?'

'We've been through this before. It all boils down to jealousy: jealousy and a determination not to let Rosalie Rassaud marry a man who she knew was a complete rotter, even if she never had the wit to see him for what he really was, a murdering bastard.'

'I suppose so.'

'I know so . . . And now, I guess, much as I'd rather

not, I'd better think about returning home.'

'Surely you will wait to do that until you have heard if England can tell you anything about Señorita Dean's early life?'

'That evidence can't alter any of the essential facts. Doesn't matter now if it turns out that she was eight-tenths dotty from the word go. Her mental state was only relevant when West had a chance of claiming that she committed suicide because she was mentally unstable.'

'I suppose that is true.'

'But you still sound doubtful?'

'I was wondering . . . about that painting.'

'Painting? What painting?'

'The one on the easel in her studio that was not finished. The tree looked so . . . tortured that surely something very dramatic had happened to her?'

'She'll have seen the engagement in dramatic terms.'

'And the broken cazuela in her bedroom. That had not been used for anything so why was it there?'

'Because she dropped it, carrying it from somewhere to somewhere else.'

'It was a large one, of the kind that is normally used only for cooking. Why should she have carried a cooking cazuela in her bedroom?'

'God knows! But don't forget, she was certainly mentally odd, even if she wasn't outright dotty. I don't reckon you can question her actions quite as you would the ordinary person's.'

'Then you don't see the broken cazuela as being of any importance?'

Alvarez had spoken so seriously that Cullon subdued his instinct to answer facetiously. 'I'm positive it isn't.'

Seated behind the desk in his office, Alvarez put a hand over the mouthpiece of the telephone. He said to Cullon: 'There is a seat on a flight late this afternoon or else one tomorrow morning.'

'I'd like to hang on, but I really ought to get back as quickly as possible.'

Alvarez uncovered the mouthpiece, spoke in Spanish, and finally replaced the receiver. 'I remembered that I have not yet taken you to Parelona Beach, so I have booked you on tomorrow's plane. It is quite impossible to come to the island and not see the most beautiful beach in the world. Even your detective-inspector would understand that.'

'Old Banger? You've got the wrong impression of how his mind works.' Cullon laughed. 'But I'll tell him today's planes were all booked out and I don't suppose, suspicious bastard as he is, he'll bother to check.'

'Good. Then we will drive to Parelona after a short siesta. And in the meantime . . .' He looked at his watch. 'It is time for lunch,' he said, with evident satisfaction.

Rifle rang the guardia post at five-thirty that afternoon, when Alvarez and Cullon were lying on the sun-drenched sands of Parelona. He tried to leave a message, but no one then at the post spoke any English.

Later, after they'd returned, sun-burned and salty, Alvarez and Cullon went to the post where they heard about the abortive telephone call. Cullon telephoned Petercross divisional HQ.

'Damned if I could get anyone to understand honest-to-God plain English,' complained Rifle. 'What the hell's the matter with 'em? . . . And where the hell were you?'

'Out tying up the last few threads of the case,' replied Cullon easily.

'Oh! Does that mean you've landed West?'

'He's sewn up tighter than a Victorian daughter's drawers.'

'It's about time . . . In that case, what I have to say won't be of much account, but you'd better listen all the same. We managed to turn up an old gossip who knew the Dean family from way back: she also remembers West and describes him as a nasty boy who couldn't be trusted. Mrs Dean died very soon after Gertrude was born and her father was left to bring her up and they wandered all over the place until they settled in Wealdsham. He was arty, unsuccessful, and lived from hand to mouth. When Gertrude was still young, he boasted that he'd invented something that was going to make his fortune. Our informant has no idea what that something was, but is certain it involved using acids. Gertrude's father had warned her never to go into his workroom which he kept locked, but one day when he was out of the house she got hold of the key and took West in there and accidentally spilled a bowl of acid over his face. That's what scarred his cheek. Gertrude became quite hysterical at what she'd done and it seemed to affect her for years afterwards.

'Later, when she was adult and her father had died, she moved from Wealdsham and that's the last time our informant saw her or heard about her. She says that in her opinion Gertrude was never really normal, especially after the acid incident. She didn't make friends, except for West, and this wasn't for lack of other people trying to be friendly. She seemed just incapable of making them.'

'Poor devil,' said Cullon.

'That's it, then. By the way, what's the temperature?'

'It was thirty-five at midday, according to one bloke: that's ninety-five on an honest scale. Must be nice on the beach, provided you don't get sunburned.'

Rifle swore.

It was barely eight o'clock, yet already the morning sun was so strong that even with the windows of the car wound right down and the ventilators fully open, they were still hot. Cullon looked at the chain of mountains thrusting their crests up into the cloudless sky. 'If ever I get half a chance, I'm going to bring Tina out here for a holiday.'

'When you come, you must see us,' said Alvarez.

Cullon wanted to say that in the short time they'd known each other he'd come to like Alvarez so much that it was impossible to imagine not looking him up as soon as possible, but being an Englishman he contented himself with: 'That would be wonderful.'

They turned on to the Playa Nueva/Palma road. 'When are you going to arrest West?' Cullon asked.

'I am not certain. But since he cannot leave the island, there is no hurry.'

'Is there ever any hurry here?'

Alvarez smiled. 'Not unless you come from Madrid. Perhaps that is why so many of us live to be old.'

'I reckon the only people likely to live to be old are the ones who keep off the roads,' said Cullon as, in the middle of the road, they breasted a rise to come face to face with a Renault also in the middle.

'Some drivers do have a very poor road sense,' agreed Alvarez, as he flicked the wheel to the right and the two cars just missed each other. He sighed, looked briefly at Cullon, sighed again. 'Tim, I wonder, have you . . .' He stopped.

'Have I what?'

'Thought about West's alibi?'

'What's there to think about? He hasn't got one.'

'Why did he ask his fiancée to give him one?'

'Well, no one else was going to, that's for sure.'

'But even he, as selfish as he is, must understand what kind of a woman she is.'

Cullon said lightly: 'Something tells me we're back to those soft, soulful eyes!'

'She's a warm, caring person and above all, honest. All the things he is not. Which must be why he is so attracted to her.'

'You're pinching the plot of half the stories in the hags'

mags. Rake attracted to virgin, hoping to be reformed by virtue. Life just doesn't work that way. Either he drags her down to his level or she turns out to be frigid.'

'What I really wish to say is this. Surely he must have realized that she would not be capable of lying convincingly?'

'Hold it. You're drawing some very wrong conclusions. When I was a bachelor, I met more than one young woman who was warm and caring and pure, for all I could ever discover, and they could all lie like troopers.'

'But do you not understand? When the señora understood he was suspected of murder, it had to be inevitable that she could no longer lie convincingly: probably that she would refuse to lie at all.'

'You could be right, but if so it just goes to prove that a bloke who's rotten to the core can make bad misjudgements about people who aren't.'

'But West is clever enough to realize and allow for that. So why did he made the bad misjudgement?'

Cullon shrugged his shoulders.

'Was it not because he panicked?'

'Possibly. He'd cause enough to panic with us breathing down his neck.'

'But if he had carefully planned the murder, as he so carefully planned the murder of his wife, he would have foreseen right from the beginning that he would need an alibi. So the fact that he panicked surely must suggest that he did not plan?'

'It means that he made a mistake – and if villains never did that, we'd hardly arrest one. How much more proof of the murder d'you need? The method was exactly the same, no one else had a motive but he had a hell of a one, his alibi's busted wide, the suicide note was typed on his machine, there wasn't a similar plastic bag in her house but there was one in his car, he'd recently had an almighty row with her . . . Even the stupidest juryman would convict without retiring.'

Alvarez said hesitantly: 'But what about the broken cazuela in her bedroom?'

'You know, I'd a feeling we might be working round to that again.'

'Why did she have a clean cooking cazuela in her bedroom?'

Cullon didn't try to answer. Alvarez concentrated on driving sufficiently fast to prevent the car behind from overtaking.

CHAPTER 21

The train drew into Petercross station and Cullon picked up his overnight case, a small parcel, and his mackintosh, and climbed down on to the platform. It was drizzling and there was no overhead canopy at this point and he hurriedly pulled on his mackintosh. It was difficult to appreciate that little more than five and a half hours earlier he'd been sweating in blazing sunshine.

Together with the other passengers who'd disembarked, he climbed the concrete stairs up to the booking hall which straddled the lines. He handed in his ticket, turned to the right and saw Tina a second before she hugged him.

They crossed to the stairs leading down to the car park. 'You're as brown as a berry and looking all relaxed,' she said. 'The holiday's obviously done you a power of good.'

'Holiday? Do you mind? I've been having to work all the hours God made.'

'Then how come you got so brown in the sun?'

He laughed. 'Strictly between you and me, maybe I did manage a little time off . . . Tina, it's a beautiful island. Forget all those stories about concrete jungles: if you know where to go, it's fantastic! I've sworn a blood oath

that you and I are going out there together just as soon as
old Banger gives me the time off he promised.'

'This is one oath I'm going to see you keep, come hell or
high water . . . Tell me, how did the work go?'

'I got the case sorted out in the end. And Enrique — he's
the local split I was working with — was a wonderful bloke,
even if he didn't have a clue about what he was supposed
to be doing.'

'He didn't?'

'Without a word of exaggeration, from beginning to
end I had to lead him by the hand and show him what to
do and how to do it.'

'I hope you were tactful about it all?'

'You know me.'

'That's why I'm asking.'

'I was tact personified. He'd no idea I was gently
prodding him along. And I left everything so he can claim
all the credit. If he lives long enough.'

'Why on earth d'you say that?'

'Every time he gets behind the wheel of a car, the
accident statistics come alive.'

At the foot of the stairs, they crossed a small lobby and
then went out on to the pavement. The car park faced
them. 'The car's right over on the other side,' she said.
'I'm afraid I couldn't park any nearer than that.'

They walked through the drizzle to the car and she
handed him the keys. He settled behind the wheel,
yawned, then yawned again, even more heavily.

'Are you worn right out with all that travelling?' she
asked solicitously.

'It's not really that. The thing is, the seats in the plane
were squashed so closely together my knees were almost
up to my chin and I just couldn't get my usual siesta.'

She stared at him with wide-eyed amazement.

They sat in the second room, which acted as both dining-room and family sitting-room. From the kitchen came the sound of a clock striking the hour. 'I suppose Tim must be back by now,' said Alvarez.

Dolores was crocheting the first of two bedspreads which Isabel, in accordance with tradition, would take to her nuptial home. She briefly looked up. 'I liked Tim a lot, but . . .'

'But what?'

Her fingers plied crochet hook and yarn. 'It's just that he sometimes seemed . . . Well, I couldn't help getting the impression that he was being condescending.'

'Condescending about what? You don't mean your cooking, do you? When he said he'd never eaten anything like it before, he was being really complimentary, not . . .'

'I'm not talking about my cooking. He could have criticized that as much as he liked.'

He did not challenge that obvious lie.

'Enrique, he was being condescending towards you in your job.'

'D'you really reckon so? . . . I suppose, if you think about it, he's entitled to be like that. After all, I haven't had a tenth of his experience.'

'That doesn't matter. You're every bit as clever as him and he'd no right to laugh at you.'

'You're imagining things.'

'I am not. Was he so very clever?' she asked challengingly.

He spoke thoughtfully. 'He certainly was quick and efficient. But sometimes he wouldn't allow himself enough time to sit down and think . . . And that's why I reckon that in the end he was wrong.'

'Did you tell him that?'

'I tried to, but he couldn't seem to understand what I was getting at.'

'Then you let him go away from here certain he's so much cleverer than you, when he just isn't?'

'I couldn't tell him straight out he was wrong, could I? After all, he was our guest.'

She did not pursue the matter. Even in her most imperious mood, she would never dream of flouting the laws of hospitality.

There was a silence, which he broke. 'I suppose I'd better make a move.'

'Where are you going?'

'Out,' he answered vaguely.

Once seated in his car, he did not immediately start the engine. He'd said to Cullon that he didn't really understand the meaning of justice. Cullon had clearly never suffered such a problem: for him, justice was the identification, arrest, conviction, and punishment, of the guilty. But how could one always be certain what was guilt? Guilt was fashioned by the current sense of morality and defined by man-made laws: morals altered not only throughout the ages, but also according to one's own viewpoint, and man could legislate wisely or stupidly . . . Who could ever convincingly answer the question, Did the starving man who took a crust of bread commit theft?

He sighed. If only Cullon had been less certain, they could have talked over the problem: but Cullon had been unable ever to see that there might be a problem.

He finally started the engine and drove away, to leave the village over the torrente. At the cross-roads he went straight over, to continue on to Ca'n Absel and as he approached the house, West stepped out on to the patio. Was West guilty or innocent of Gertrude Dean's death? It all depended on how you defined guilt.

West's face was drawn and, despite the suntan, there were dark bags under his eyes, suggesting worry and a sleepless night: the scarring on his right cheek was unusually pronounced. 'Where's the other bloke?'

'Señor Cullon? He has returned to England: I drove him to the airport earlier on.'

'I call that good riddance.'

Alvarez brought a handkerchief from his pocket and mopped the sweat from his face. 'Could we move into the shade before I ask a few questions?'

'More? Christ, d'you get paid by the score? Why don't you start asking intelligent questions, like what really happened when Gertie died?'

'As to that, I believe I now know.'

West, his expression strained, stared at him for several seconds, then abruptly he turned and led the way across to the patio chairs. He slammed his clenched fist down on the table. 'Well? What d'you know?'

Alvarez sat, then said gravely: 'Why did you tell Señora Rassaud you were going out on the Monday night the señorita died, when you knew you were to stay in your house?'

'Isn't it obvious? I didn't want Rosalie here.'

'Why not?'

West finally sat. 'Do I have to spell everything out? It was because Gertie had said she was coming to see me here . . . And then she never bloody well turned up.'

'You still have not explained why you did not wish the two ladies to meet? After all, they were friends.'

'Not by then.'

'According to Señor Meade they were still friends, if not as friendly as they had once been.'

'Forget what he says. When he's sober he's a liar, when he's drunk he'll swear blind he's got four heads.'

'The señora has herself said she was still friendly with the señorita.'

'We're just not on the same wavelength, are we? To begin with, they liked each other right enough, but Gertie was the possessive kind: if she was friendly with you, you mustn't become as friendly with anyone else. When Rosalie and I got engaged, Gertie became ridiculously jealous and kept creating scenes.'

'Was not your real reason for keeping them apart the fact that you did not want the señora to hear the señorita say that you had murdered your wife?'

'I didn't murder Babs. How many more times do I have to goddamn well say that?'

'When you were young, you lived in the same town as the señorita. You were with her when your face became scarred. Which of you suggested going into the locked room?'

'She did.'

'This time, the truth.'

West hesitated. 'I can't remember. It's a hell of a long time ago.'

'It surely was you who made the suggestion?'

'I . . . Well, maybe I could have done.'

'Who picked up the bowl of acid?'

'She did.'

'Why can you still not understand? The time for lying is over, unless you wish to be convicted of the señorita's murder . . . It was you who picked up the bowl, was it not?'

West said sullenly: 'What if it was?'

'You spilled the acid over yourself. Yet you told everyone it was her fault.'

'That was a joke.'

'You can call it a joke?'

'I didn't know she was going to take it so seriously.'

'Just how seriously did she take it?'

'What are you getting at now?'

'I am trying to understand how she felt, because if I can understand that I think I shall know what really happened when she died . . . Did she feel guilty for the injuries she believed she had caused you? So guilty that she was convinced she owed you a debt which could never be repaid?'

West didn't answer.

'And when she grew old enough to realize that she could not be held responsible by anyone, least of all herself, for what she thought she had done when young, what happened then?'

'Nothing.'

'What happened?' demanded Alvarez angrily.

'She . . . she just used to hang around.'

'Because her sense of guilt had become a need to serve, which in turn had become love?'

'Goddamn it, I wouldn't know.'

'A man like you would always know. And take advantage of his knowledge . . . You left the neighbourhood. When did you next see her?'

West shrugged his shoulders.

'I have told you, I believe the truth will help you — but I cannot know the truth about Señorita Dean's death until I know the truth about her life. When did you next see her?'

'I can't give you chapter and verse,' he said sullenly. 'It was when she'd begun to paint for a living.'

'Where was she living at that time?'

'In a flat on the outskirts of Wealdsham.'

'And you began to live with her?'

'What if I did? She was over the age of consent.'

'But not beyond the age of dreams. She had loved you and now she believed that you must love her because you were living with her. So what do you imagine she believed when you left her?'

'I've . . . I've no idea.'

'You have a very good idea. Did you see her again before you married?'

'No.'

'Did you tell her you were married. Or did you leave her to learn this from someone else?'

'I suppose she must have heard it from someone else.'

'Did the news upset her?'

'I wasn't there, so I can't tell, can I?'

'Perhaps, since she could be certain you had not married for love, she was not as upset as she might have been.'

West flushed.

'What was the acid in?'

For a moment, he was confused by the reference to what they had been discussing earlier. Then he said: 'That all happened nearly thirty years back. I haven't the faintest idea.'

'Was it in an earthenware dish?'

'In case you weren't listening, I've just said, I can't remember.'

'I think it must have been . . . When did she learn that it was not she who was responsible for scarring you and giving you such pain? It was yourself.'

'I've no idea.'

'It was very shortly before she died, was it not? And that was when for the very first time, she could see you as the person you really are: someone incapable of being concerned with anyone but himself. And the moment she could understand that, she could also understand that you must have murdered your wife and then tricked her into giving you the alibi which enabled you to escape arrest.'

'I didn't kill Babs,' West shouted. He again slammed a clenched fist down on the table.

'The señorita came to live on the island to escape from life and from you. And by all accounts, miraculously she succeeded. And among her friends was Señora Rassaud with whom her friendship reached an intensity that could be called, depending on your way of looking at things, either unusually intense or abnormal . . . It is not difficult to understand why, after so many years of emotional starvation.

'The news of your engagement must have shocked her,

partly because of her former feelings towards you, but
mainly because she was in a position to judge that the
señora was far too good a person for you. That shock was
magnified beyond bearing when she understood the
truth—that your wife had been murdered by you. Now,
her greatest friend was to be married to a murderer . . .
She threatened you, trying to make you give up the
marriage, didn't she? What was that threat: to tell the
English police the truth?'

'She was hysterical, nothing more. I said I was going to
marry Rosalie and there was absolutely nothing she could
do about it.'

'So she proved you wrong. There was just one way in
which she could prevent the marriage and at the same
time punish you for all the terrible harm you'd caused to
others—and, ironically, it was you who'd shown her how
to do this. You had disguised a murder as suicide. She
would disguise her own suicide as murder.'

There was a silence, broken only by the shrilling of
cicadas.

'She . . . she did commit suicide after all?' demanded
West.

'Yes.'

'Christ!' His voice rose. 'If she committed suicide, you
can't touch me?'

'Provided it can be proved, no.'

'Then pull your finger out and prove it.'

'Some of the proof is already to hand. The señorita
made one or two mistakes. She used a proposed change
in her will to suggest a motive for her murder, just as your
wife's will had suggested the motive, but who can
seriously believe that you, now a very wealthy man, would
have murdered the señorita for the relatively small
amount of money she had? She committed suicide in
exactly the same way in which your wife was supposed to
have done because that in itself would arouse suspicion:

but she even went so far as to choose the same time and surely you would not have done that because if suspicion were once aroused, such a coincidence would reinforce this.

'She bought a typewriter a few days before she died — but why should she suddenly buy a typewriter when she had such little correspondence? And since you had not seen her after the beginning of the month, how could you know, if you were the murderer, that now you could type out the suicide note on your own machine and make it look genuine, provided only that an expert did not closely study it?

'She was careful to spend part of the last Sunday with Señor Meade and to be so gay and cheerful that he would immediately claim she could not have committed suicide. But it is clear that she was unnaturally cheerful. Why, unless there were good reason?

'But if she made mistakes, she still planned very carefully and this makes it difficult to prove the truth. She was careful to use a plastic bag of a different size from any in the house. She typed out the suicide note on your machine.' Alvarez was silent for a moment, then he said: 'When, in the past three weeks, did she come to this house?'

'I've told you, I didn't see her because she didn't turn up.'

'Of course not. That arrangement — which you were bound to honour because you were scared — was to make certain you had no alibi. Nevertheless, there was a time, wasn't there, when she did visit this house and you were not here?'

At first, West's expression remained blank, then it suddenly became excited. 'Goddamn it, she was here roughly a fortnight ago! Francisca told me about it the next day.'

'Where were you?'

'Out on my yacht, with Rosalie . . . That's when she used my typewriter to make the suicide note!'

Alvarez thought about the receipt for the new typewriter which had been among Gertrude's papers. Yet the laboratory report on the suicide note had referred to worn lettering. A man of sharper intelligence would have begun to understand the truth then . . . 'Which car did you drive down to the port?'

'The Seat, because I don't like leaving the Mercedes unattended for too long these days . . . By God, that's how she planted the plastic bag in the Merc!'

Alvarez nodded.

West smacked his right fist into the palm of his left hand. 'It's taken you a goddamn age to uncover the truth.'

'I am afraid that for a long time I could not appreciate the meaning of some things, especially the unfinished painting and the cazuela.'

'What are you on about now?'

'The olive tree in the painting was full of torment. Why? Because she had been forced to realize that the man she had once loved had in reality always despised her and was responsible for twisting her life out of shape: that the only way in which to save Señora Rassaud was to kill herself and make it look like murder.'

'She was twice round the bloody twist.'

'And then there was the cazuela. Just before she lay down on her bed to kill herself, she smashed the earthenware cazuela on the floor of the bedroom.'

'Where was that supposed to get her?'

Alvarez looked at him. 'It was a symbolic gesture: a way of gaining her freedom.'

'I don't know what the hell you're talking about.'

'Then nothing I can say will ever manage to explain it to you.'

West showed his baffled anger. 'All right, so she tried

hard. But it didn't bloody work. I'm as free as the breeze. So now we're going to have a bit of a celebration. Champagne all right?'

'Nothing for me.'

He shrugged his shoulders, stood, went into the house. When he returned, he carried two glasses and a frosting bottle of champagne. He set one of the glasses in front of Alvarez. 'I reckon you'll change your mind quickly enough when the stuff's in front of you.'

'Please understand, I do not wish to have a drink with you.'

'Suit yourself. Suddenly become very choosey? Drunk enough of my booze before now. What's eating you? Furious because you were hoping to run me in?' He opened the bottle and filled his glass, careless when the bubbling champagne overflowed on to the table. 'It's just your bad luck if thinking about it gives you ulcers. I didn't kill Gertie and there's not a thing you can do about it.'

'You may be correct, but if so it will be only after it is quite certain there is sufficient proof of your innocence.'

'Come off it! You've already had to admit there is.'

'I have explained that I know the truth, because where I can't be certain of something, I have assumed what the truth most probably is. But in a court of law, things are different—as you know, having taken advantage of this fact to escape the consequences of murdering your wife. There, nothing may be assumed, everything must be proved. And the facts surrounding the señorita's death seem to prove she was murdered by someone who tried to disguise her murder as suicide. It is only when one understands the whole of the señorita's life and her relationship with you that one is able to understand that she had sufficient motive to commit suicide and try to make it appear that you had murdered her.'

'So?' he demanded carelessly. He drank.

'You will not legally be able to establish your innocence unless you are ready to admit to all of the truth, in
particular to the fact that the señorita gave you a false
alibi on the night on which your wife was murdered.'

Slowly, West lowered his glass. Admit that and he
would be extradited to England, to be tried and found
guilty of the murder of Babs. Refuse to admit it and he
would be tried on the island for the murder of Gertrude
and, because she had learned so well the lesson he had
taught her, be found guilty . . .